JOSEPH
AND THE
SEVEN
SWORDS

FAISAL ALOTHAINAH

JOSEPH
AND THE
SEVEN
SWORDS

TABLE OF CONTENTS

FOREWORD

One day, one of us will be a scientist, an artist, a doctor, or a policymaker...One day, one of us will make a positive impact on this earth... One day, one of us will make a difference in the world...

The current generation was born in an era of technology, mass communication, and social distance. Although the world is becoming more and more technologically sophisticated, we are beginning to distance ourselves from what makes us fundamentally human. As humans, we are still forgetful, emotional, and take the path of least resistance. Technology is managing to profit from these human traits. We have created many tools meant to make life better, but there are underlying consequences to this new relationship with technology.

Technology and social networks are what is mostly driving consumerism in modern society. This is not the kind of consumerism of times past. This is a narrowing of culture. As we all become exposed to the same information, we all begin to want the same items, the same things, and the same objects. In fact, the narrower the scope our consumeristic desires become, the more our freedom of choice is devalued. We all want the same thing because we are sold to want it, does this choice matter? I would say it does.

As a society, we are drawn to chase short-term reward rather than long term goals. The result is, we sacrifice our dreams and our destiny for instant gratification. If we want to make our dreams a reality, we need to shift our attention to ourselves, to our own self-discovery. Technology is only a distraction from the work of making our lives bigger and better.

I do believe that each of us has a purpose and a message in our soul. All we need is a little spark of inspiration to bring it out. We need a good story to inspire us. When people have heard a story of someone who has started their life from the ground up, it might motivate them to keep going on their dream. If someone could do it, then maybe just maybe you can too. What about giving the world a story that would help them to discover their life's purpose. With a story like that in hand, what could the next generation become?

I do believe that we are lucky to live in an era so full of knowledge. But perhaps it's too much knowledge? We now know that what is needed is not just more knowledge, but also more experience. As Winston Churchill famously said, "those who fail to learn from history are condemned to repeat it."

It is only the accumulation of human experiences that make us all better people. This is the driving force behind this book. It is what compels me to share my experiences with my generation. If each of us shared his/her experiences in life, I believe that humanity would evolve in ways that better serve the common good. This sharing of knowledge leads us to self-discovery. I have made many mistakes in life, and I don't wish others to repeat them. I imagine that you, too, may have made mistakes in your life that you do not wish for me to repeat. Sharing our common experiences helps make this possible.

I embarked upon my own journey of self-discovery at the young age of eleven. I have always encountered teachers, tutors, and coaches everywhere I go. I seek out knowledge, original ideas, and a new approach to life. This is what made me travel the world in search of my own life philosophy. What I seek is the truth. I am aware that no one person can hold the ultimate truth, but I am on a path of discovery. I am in search of my own truth, my own purpose, and my own philosophy *Inshallah* (In Arabic means: God willing). Amazingly despite years of searching, it was in the process of writing this novel that I began to know myself at an even deeper level than ever before. In fact, I got to know myself better than thru ten years of attending seminars, courses, workshops, or even Ted-talks! I discovered one thing. To discover yourself is to return to yourself.

The main character in the book *Joseph* appeared to me in my mind's eye, and I decided to follow him to see where we would go together. The deeper I went, the more mystery I revealed about myself. The deeper I went, the more I saw the things that were just beneath the surface. Until joseph showed me the way, I was unaware of these hidden secrets. It is at moments like this that you can either deny or embrace what you learn about yourself. If you choose to embrace what you find, you might just discover your true inner self.

What you will read in this book are words that I sourced from the heart. Walking into the unknown is a terrifying thing, *but why do we so often avoid the unknown? Are we scared to go into the shadows of ourselves?* The mind is a powerful force. If you have this strength mind, you can stay in prison for 30 years and feel happy, go off to distant lands, and feel at home. In contrast, if you have yet to discover this power, you may enter a place full of people and feel totally alone or go only to your friend's house and feel homesick. My hope is that this book will take you on a journey of your own self-discovery.

I never thought that one day I would publish a novel. To be honest, I had no idea, but I decided to give it a shot. Day by day, the story began to unfold until *Joseph* met the *seven warriors.* During the writing of the story, questions began to unfold in my mind that needed answering. But by the end of the tale, my questions had fundamentally changed. *Why do we fear the future? Why do we not surrender ourselves to the calling?* People sometimes don't like the idea that we cannot control our fate, but the question needs to be asked, *have you discovered your fate?* You may never know what your fate is, but I genuinely believe that sometimes there will be some clues along the way that will help you to understand your higher purpose in this life.

What I hope is that my message will be heard, known, read, and understood throughout humanity.

This is me, and I am Faisal AlOthainah

The Sword Will Guide Him

Mr. Galvestone sat in his study, where the bookshelves reached the roof, in the Scottish castle he'd inherited from his father. The castle had so many rooms and was so huge it was possible for someone to get lost there. He'd lived in the castle for decades and it held many memories for him. Mr. Galvestone was tall with white hair and piercing black eyes over which he wore eyeglasses because his sight was diminishing with age. He was drinking a cup of herbal tea and reading a book about the Renaissance while waiting for his grandchildren to arrive.

There was a knock at the door.

The housekeeper, Miss Wingate, had worked with Mr. Galvestone's father for decades after he'd found her in a shelter at the end of World War Two. She dropped what she was doing went to open the door where she greeted the grandchildren warmly. Miss Wingate had already prepared a plate of fruits from the garden located in the back of the castle for them.

"Mr. Galvestone, your grandchildren have arrived," called Miss Wingate.

Mr. Galvestone replied, "I've missed them. Take them to the sitting room. I'll be there in a moment."

"As you wish, Mr. Galvestone."

He finished reading the page he was on, put the book down, and made his way to the sitting room. Mr. Galvestone liked to sit there with his grandchildren in his castle where he lived a pleasant and peaceful life surrounded by nature. He had five grandchildren: Claire the oldest was eleven and liked history much as her grandfather did, Sophia was nine and artistic. The twins Lewis and Patrick were seven and studious. Charlotte – Mr. Galvestone's favorite – was five.

They loved their grandfather because he played games with them and told them stories. After his wife Margaret had died of cancer many years earlier, Mr. Galvestone had lost interest in life. He'd felt lonely without a sense of purpose – spending time with his grandchildren revived him. Mr. Galvestone had been an archeologist. He'd studied archeology for many years. It was his passion, and he'd loved reading about history while traveling around the world and conducting research.

His grandchildren liked to explore every room in the castle while the housekeeper ran after them, making sure they didn't break any of their grandfather's valuables such as paintings, old documents, and Louis XV furniture. When the sky darkened, his grandchildren surrounded Mr. Galvestone as he sat on his weathered leather chair beside the fire.

"Grandfather, why do you have white hair?" asked Charlotte.

"That's is what happens when you get old. You'll have white hair one day."

Lewis looked around curiously and pointed at the spot on the wall where a well-used, ancient sword hung. He said, "Grandfather, you promised us you'd tell us the sword's story. Can you tell us it now?"

Mr. Galvestone tried to remember everything he knew about the sword. "It's an ancient story called *Joseph and the Seven Swords.*"

The grandchildren grinned and said, "We want to hear it!"

Mr. Galvestone called to Miss Wingate, "Could you bring milk and biscuits for the kids? I'm going to tell them an ancient and meaningful story."

"As you wish, Mr. Galvestone."

Mr. Galvestone began.

~ ~ ~

In the faraway Kingdom of Zelaar, King Edmund was about to attend a reception and greet guests from another kingdom. It was an important meeting because the King wanted to improve relations with the other kingdom as they had been fighting for a decade. This meeting was intended to end the conflict between the two nations. King Edmund was waiting in the main hall because he expected the delegation to arrive at any second.

At the same time, the King's wife, Queen Amelia, had gone into labor, The pains were so intense that she knew she would soon give birth. A servant went to see the Professor, the King's adviser, to tell him.

"Thank you for informing me," said the Professor. "I'll deliver the message to the King."

When the Professor told the King, Edmund said, "What? Now? Amelia is giving birth? I can't go right now. You go instead of me. Once I've finished I'll be there."

The Professor was the most trusted person in the castle because he'd long worked for the King and his father before him. He was responsible for ensuring royal protocol was always observed. As he was walking to another building to check on the Queen, he saw that the moon was aglow, burning red in the night sky. *We see a royal castle glowing red from the light of the blood moon. We hear a woman screaming with pain*, he said to himself. This was a sign that a new king was coming to life – and not just any king. A righteous king who would claim his ancestors' power.

The Professor attempted to hide his emotions because when he conveyed the prophecy of the red moon omen to the Queen, she would feel sorrow because of having to sacrifice one of her children. He decided to return to the main hall to ask the chief guard to accompany him. Together they went to the Queen and watched her for a moment before she realized they'd arrived. Queen Amelia was gazing out of the window at the glowing moon. Her midwife and a maid stood alongside her. The Professor sensed that although the Queen was in pain, she was also happy to be soon giving birth, and she was filled with sorrow because of the sacrifice she needed to make.

"Your Highness," said the Professor.

In a sad voice she said, "Do I need to do it?"

"Your Highness, you know you must. We don't know what is in your womb, but you need to sacrifice it because the prophecy says that at a red moon the Queen should sacrifice her boy or the older son if she has a twin."

The Queen didn't answer so the Professor repeated, "You must."

~ ~ ~

The Queen gave birth to twins – a boy and a girl. She feared for their lives because she hadn't believed this prophecy would apply to her child. Amelia had thought the glowing red moon was a myth – the last time it happened had been more than a century before. She thought it was a story that old people used to tell their children, even though the Professor who observed all the norms was the first to witness it in disbelief. Amelia could see how powerless he felt and that he didn't want to accept the prophecy.

It had been a hard and difficult labor. The Queen feared she might die – if that happened, the king would marry another woman to bear him a son to be the next king. *But I can't sacrifice my son*, she thought.. *Who would the future queen be? What sort of stepmother would she be for my children?*

But the Professor insisted that the Queen gave the boy child away and asked her maid to send him with one of the loyal knights. So Amelia sacrificed her son's future and sent him away for his own protection. As she lay there, the Queen was losing more and more blood and becoming weaker while the maids, the Chief of Guards, and the Professor witnessed helplessly.

"I thought I would die and I never thought the prophecy was real," said the Queen.

"Your Highness, you need to have faith in the prophecy," said the Professor, "and believe that the sword will find, prepare and guide the future king to receive his rightful inheritance. The Chief of Guards will take charge of sending your boy away"

"But –"

"Your Highness," the Professor interrupted, "the old Zelaarian prophecy said: *When the red moon rises and twins are born, the first-born shall be sacrificed or the future shall be forlorn*"

The Queen said through her pain, "Open the closet and you will find money for the task at hand."

"Your wish is my command, Your Majesty."

The Queen ordered the Professor to give one of the loyal knights money and a sword and ordered him to go to a faraway place. Shortly after, the King – after finishing the reception – went to his wife and saw one child and that she was a girl. He called her Isabella.

Amelia's maid whispered to her, "Why did you give the sword to the knight?"

The Queen responded, "The sword will guide him."

A few hours later she was dead.

~ ~ ~

In a village in a valley, there lived a boy called Joseph who was eleven years old. Joseph cared for everyone around him. He helped his father while cultivating plants and went to the market every day, saying hello to everyone from the butcher to the grocery man. Joseph was so well-respected that all the villagers wanted to spend time with him – he was a good listener. Joseph never felt bored when listening to others because he could put himself in their stories and feel what they felt. He could see the good in everyone he met and could show them how to embrace their good traits by shifting their focus onto who they truly were.

Joseph and his friend Albert argued all the time about anything and everything. They had a close bond and met regularly, although not every day. Once a while, they liked going to peaceful places to retreat from reality, to relax and read their books, to hunt and fish if they so desired. Their favorite spot was near a peaceful and quiet lake where they went once a week at sunset. There, they could sit and talk about their lives and dreams.

Joseph had lots of dreams and his altruistic spirit guided him to make a positive impact on any place he entered. Albert was the only one who listened to him carefully without interruption. Joseph gained his strength from people who believed in him.

One day Joseph asked Albert, "What do you think the meaning of life is?"

"That's too big a thing to be covered in one sentence. What do you think it is, Joseph?"

"To be honest, I don't know, but I'm willing to seek answers even if it takes the rest of my life."

"When you find them, please share them with me." Albert laughed.

"See our surroundings. This is life, Albert. Life is static and doesn't change. Just like that bird –" Joseph pointed "– every day he does the same things, so life is a pattern. Life repeats itself every day."

Albert laughed again. "Well, now, I am sure you are my friend Joseph. Who but you would talk about things that I don't understand?"

It was late and almost dark and so time to go home. Once he'd arrived home, Joseph went to the second person in the world who always listened to him talk about his dreams – his mother. Every night he talked to his mother about his day, life, and his dreams until she fell asleep. Usually, mothers go to their child's bed and tell them stories, but with Joseph, it was the opposite.

One rainy night, he went to the storeroom, searching for wood to take inside the cottage. When he entered he saw something gleaming in the corner, so he went closer. It was covered with a piece of cloth, and when he lifted the cloth he saw something sharp, metal, and dusty. He wasn't sure what it was at first but it seemed someone had hidden it. It was an ancient sword.

Full of curiosity, he felt an urge to touch it. He took the piece of cloth that was covering the sword and wrapped it around himself. In his mind, he was a knight and he started playing and jumping around some trees, forgetting that his family needed the wood to get warm. Suddenly the sword sparked and vibrated and this panicked him. Then he heard whispers calling his name, "Joseph, Joseph, Joseph."

Suddenly, seven warriors appeared, surrounding him in a circle. They told him "Don't be afraid."

He threw the sword aside and it lost its spark. Then Joseph ran back to his cottage and told his mother what had happened. He was scared because of what he'd seen and thought it was an illusion.

His mother had known this day would come but she remained silent, stroking his hair, assuring him that nothing bad would happen.

Day by day, Joseph became more mature, stronger, sharper, and more handsome. One day, while he was walking in the forest, he came across the sword and played with it again. The sword sparked and the seven warriors appeared. He panicked again but this time was brave and stood his ground, asking them, "Who are you?"

One warrior said, "We are here to help you get back your throne because you are the king."

Again, Joseph thought he was delusional. He threw the sword away.

While lying in bed that night, he laughed about what the warrior had said. *Am I a king?* His sister Miriam came to him and asked why he was laughing. He told her about the sword and the seven warriors.

Miriam laughed and said, "How can you be the king and also my twin?"

"Yes, it makes no sense."

"Either you're the king or you're my brother."

He couldn't get what had happened to him out of his mind and he started to hear the whispering again and again. The thought that this event had occurred twice in his life made Joseph jump from his bed as soon as Mariam had gone and make his way stealthily to the forest. He went to the sword and grabbed it. Suddenly, the sword began to spark and the seven warriors surrounded him.

"Who are you? And what do you want from me?" he asked.

"We are here to help you," said one of the warriors.

"Why do you want to help me? You aren't real and I'm not the king."

"Yes, you are, but you are not aware of it."

"How can I be the king? I'm only a farmer," Joseph said.

"You are Queen Amelia's son and King Edmund is your father."

"But if my mother was the Queen, why did she send me away?"

"Your mother sacrificed you because she was obeying the prophecy," the warrior said.

"What prophecy?"

"The old Zelaarian prophecy said: *When the red moon rises, and if two twins are born, the first-born shall be sacrificed or the future shall be forlorn*"

"But how come I'm here?" asked Joseph. "And why are you appearing to me now?"

"The night your mother sent you away, a loyal knight was given the task of taking you to a farmer – your current family. A sword and a lot of money were used to convince them to take you. The farmer accepted the deal while his wife was giving birth to her own little girl."

"Why my mother, the Queen, gave the knight the sword?"

"She knew that the King's sword would guide you on your journey to get back your throne."

Joseph asked in shock, "Do you mean that I will be king after my father dies?"

"Joseph," the warrior said gently, "your purpose in life is to be King of Zelaar. We will assist you in your journey to retrieve your rightful inheritance and fulfill your destiny. But before your journey will start, you need to learn a few things."

"What things?"

"You will find out. Just follow the signs."

"How will I know if I don't already know?"

"You need to figure it out, but to know that you know, you need to ask yourself questions."

Joseph said impatiently, "So what's next? How will I get back my throne?"

"You will know. You need to move to the city."

Joseph wanted to ask more questions but the warriors disappeared before he had a chance.

He went to his mother and asked if what he'd been told was true.

She nodded and said, "I got used to you although you aren't my true-born son. You are the son I didn't have and fate had sent you to me. If you feel you need to do anything to get back your throne, I will pray to God to save you from danger."

His mother hugged him. She'd realized that hiding that sword had given her time to spend time with him, but as humans, we only can postpone fate – we can't stop it.

Joseph put the sword under his bed, frustrated that he didn't yet know what he should do, but he was sure he'd receive a sign. Eleven nights later, he felt the sword starting to vibrate and spark. Now was the time to accept his call and chase his destiny. He grabbed a small leather bag, packed his things and, carrying the sword, he said goodbye to his family. When Miriam cried at the thought of Joseph leaving, she gave him a small bracelet so he would remember her. she said, "When you become king, make me a duchess."

Joseph accepted some money from his father to go to the city – it was approximately six hours away by foot. While he was heading to the city, he stopped under a big tree to take a nap. Suddenly, he awoke, conscious that someone was nearby. He opened his eyes and saw a stranger pointing his sword between his eyes.

Joseph panicked, and said, "What do you want from me?"

"How come a person like you own a sword like this? Are you a thief?"

"It's a long story," said Joseph, "my mother gave it to me."

"Is your mother the Queen?"

"Yes – and you don't believe me."

"Of course I don't believe you."

Joseph said petulantly, "As your future king, I order you to put the sword aside and follow my orders."

"Well, my lord, if I kill you now, no-one will know!"

Then, the sword vibrated. It sparked and in fear the stranger threw it aside. Joseph took the sword and pointed it at the stranger's head. "If I kill you now, no-one will know," he said.

"You have proved your point."

Joseph held out his hand to the stranger and said, "My name is Joseph."

"My name is Thomas."

"It's nice to meet you, Thomas. What do you do for a living?"

"I work in the circus. We're traveling between cities and stayed in this area last night. While I was out walking, I saw you under this tree having a nap. What about you?"

"I'm heading to the city but I don't know what's next," Joseph replied:

"We're heading to the city," said Thomas. "Would you like to join us?"

"Yes, I would."

Thomas walked with Joseph to the area where the circus had placed their tents. While Joseph was walking to an enormous tent, he saw many people with monkeys and other animals and people with tattoos. It was a pleasant experience for him to see a new world and new animals such elephants, lions and various birds. They went to a massive tent to grab food. Here a man was practicing his fire show, and others were playing with some birds. For Joseph, it was like fantasy, and he immersed himself in it. Thomas introduced Joseph to his friends, and they ate and rested. When it was time for dinner, Joseph had fallen asleep so the circus family decided to wake him up. They planned a welcoming ceremony to share their joy in life with him. Thomas made the arrangements and asked the monkey's trainer to send a monkey with him to wake Joseph.

Some of the members of the circus surrounded Joseph and he began to wake up. Then the party began.

Joseph opened his eyes. "What's going on?" he asked. "And why is there a monkey wearing a costume and holding a knife?"

Then he heard a parrot saying, "Party time, my lord."

A few muscular men led Joseph by the hand to the ceremony. Joseph was shocked by what was happening to him, and he thought he was in a dream. They headed to the bonfire where a lamb was grilling and people were singing. Suddenly, someone flashed fire from his mouth. Joseph felt amazed and smiled at the thought of the help Thomas had given him.

While Joseph was eating, he saw a woman sitting with her cards. He asked Thomas, "What does that woman do?"

"You don't know what that is? Well, it will be fun. Come with me. Don't be afraid."

They went to the Oracle and asked her to do a reading for Joseph. The woman replied, "You need to pay."

Joseph asked, "How much will it cost?"

"You need to pay me a third of what you have now."

"That's too much."

"Take it or leave it. I can tell you something that will teach you a lot because you are at the beginning of your journey and you need to learn many things."

Joseph remembered what the seven warriors told him about learning new things, so he calculated that a third would not be that much if he was to be king.

Thomas said, "Come on, it will be fun."

Joseph gave the Oracle a third of his money, and she asked him to enter the tent. Once inside, and in the warm, he saw a lot of bottles and things he didn't recognize which made him feel scared, such as bottles with scorpions, snakes, and a fish skeleton. The woman shuffled the cards and showed him three cards.

"The first card shows me that a handsome man is drinking poison," she said.

"What does that mean?"

"If someone will destroy you, it will be you, not a stranger. Also, it means that if you are poisoned, you will be the only one who can cure yourself – it should start with you."

Joseph said to Thomas in shock and panic, "I'm not sure if I want her to continue her reading!"

"Don't be afraid," Thomas said.

"We're on the second card," the Oracle said.

Thomas said to Joseph, "It's okay."

"This card shows someone in a hole and their stairway leading out to the dark hole with a missing step. Outside that hole is a huge castle," the Oracle said.

"What does that mean?" Joseph asked.

The Oracle looked into Joseph's eyes and said, "This card hasn't appeared to me for a few years – and now I am starting to worry about you! What will happen to you, you need to face alone."

"Is it dangerous?"

"I can't see exactly what's the future is hiding for you. Let me turn over the third card."

The third card showed two horses looking at each other, one black and one white.

"What does that mean?" asked Joseph.

"When you find yourself, you will find your twin flame, but to find yourself you need to embrace yourself and be aware of yourself."

"Is it beautiful?" Joseph asked.

"Your souls were one soul!"

After they finished the reading, the woman gave him a bottle of liquid telling him to drink it when he was alone. After that, he went to the sleeping tent and rested well.

In the morning, the caravans headed in the direction of the city, spending one more night in a place fifty miles away. Joseph had a pleasant lunch with his new friend Thomas and they sat under a tree and talked.

"So, you the king, huh?" Thomas asked.

"It's a long story, and I don't know how to get back my throne – and I don't know it if I'll be a good king."

"I wish I could give you advice on how to be a good king but I've never been a king!"

Joseph smiled and said, "I feel I need to do something but I don't know what to do."

"It might sound crazy," said Thomas, "but when I want to do something, I do it without thinking."

"But to be a king, you need to take your time because many people lean on you."

"Let me tell you what I learned from the circus," Thomas said. "To perform well in the circus, you need to flow with the rhythm of other movements without letting them disrupt your performance. When we perform, we feel that we are one – not separate".

"It seems you are a wise man! How come you're in the circus?"

"You know the Oracle?"

"Yes, what about her?"

"She's my mother, but we don't talk with each other and try to keep our distance. You shouldn't trust her, and you need to throw the liquid away she gave you."

"But you urged me to go to her in the first place," Joseph said. "Why?"

"It was business. I try to keep my relationship with her businesslike and I had intended to share your third with her, but now I don't want to because I know who you are. Again, you shouldn't drink that liquid and don't trust my mother."

"It's okay, Thomas." Joseph paused before asking, "What you will do in the city?"

"We will stay for a while in the city because it's so huge and many people will want to see our performance. What about you?"

"I thought I knew, but I don't. I might find a job to earn a living."

The caravans were ready to go to the city, and they embarked, heading toward their destiny.

THE HYMN OF JOSEPH

The caravans arrived in the city, and you could hear the loudness of the people doing transactions with each other. The circus members embarked from the caravans to build the main tent. Joseph wanted to give them space to do their work so when he saw a small place that offered food, he went there to eat lunch and ordered a small sandwich. Two people were talking loudly and he heard them they say that the King had become sick and couldn't run the country

"At the last reception, the King wasn't in good shape," the first man said.

"There's a rumor he's started to forget his family's names. I'm not sure if he can run the country," said the second.

"I heard he might die soon because he's so sick."

Joseph gulped. This was his father and he felt upset because he thought he might not have the chance to say goodbye to him. He finished his meal and returned to the circus to see they'd set up the tents and went to his friend Thomas.

"How was your lunch?" asked Thomas.

"It was good."

"Wait a second, you look upset! Why? What's happened?"

"I heard people say that the King is sick and I wanted to say goodbye to him. I'm not sure if he knows he has a living son."

Thomas laughed. "I don't know if this is real or not! You seem serious and you don't seem insane to me."

"Why would I want to lie about it?"

Thomas put his hand on Joseph's shoulder and said, "I know you'll figure it out."

"I wanted to ask you if I could stay with the circus for a few days until I find a place to stay," Joseph said. "Maybe I could help you to organize the visitors to the circus?"

"Sure!"

Joseph went to the staff tent to get some rest, and the monkey came over and played with him. Joseph talked to the monkey and it seemed the monkey understood him and was trying to express his thoughts with body language. Joseph said to the monkey, "Would you like to be a king?" and the monkey mimicked Joseph's way of talking. Joseph laughed.

Later, he rested on his bed thinking about everything that had happened to him, starting with the sword and ending with when he met the Oracle. He daydreamed about the throne and his twin flame. His imagination led him to visualize many things – his future queen beside him, as his thoughts began to drift; his first date, his first vacation, deciding what he would call his first son…

The seeds the Oracle had planted in his mind made him obsess over his thoughts. He was beginning to forget he had a journey to make. Joseph remembered his best friend Albert and how he'd forced himself to not say goodbye to him and hoped that one day Albert would forgive him. If he'd met him before he started his journey, he might have had second thoughts and canceled his trip. He preferred to avoid the meeting altogether rather than say goodbye, giving Albert the opportunity to try to talk him out of his decision – and he wanted to protect Albert from feeling their friendship was over.

Thomas appeared and told Joseph that he needed his help to greet the visitors for the first show as all the tickets had been sold. Joseph went to the main entrance to collect the tickets from the guests. The entrance was crowded with people pushing each other because within a few minutes the show would start. It was here that he saw someone trying to enter the tent from the staff entrance. Joseph decided to challenge the sneak who wanted to see the show without paying and discreetly followed them. He realized the show had begun when he heard the ringmaster letting off fireworks.

The stranger was climbing the stairs to view the show from a tiny square torn in the tent.

Joseph raised his voice saying, "Who are you, and what are you doing here?"

"I can't hear you. What?" the stranger answered.

Joseph said, "What sort of a man are you that doesn't pay his entrance fee?"

"First, I'm not a man but a woman." She lowered her scarf so Joseph could see her face.

"I'm so sorry! I couldn't see your face because of the scarf."

"The view is breathtaking from this angle and it is far better to watch from here instead of amongst the crowds," she said.

Joseph remembered the Oracle's words about finding his twin flame. Perhaps this intruder might be his future queen. He politely said, "My name is Joseph. What about you, my lady?"

"Nice to meet you, Joseph, but I wouldn't be interested even if you were the king."

Joseph flexed his shoulders and said, "I am the future king – well, maybe the future king."

She looked him up and down and said, "Well, yes, now I believe you, young boy. Sorry, Your Majesty, can you please give me somewhere to see this show?"

"But I allowed you in though you paid nothing."

She looked him in his eye and said, "Royalty doesn't compromise a woman for anything." She slapped his face and went to the stairs to leave.

Joseph was shocked by what had happened. "At least let me knew your name!"

She looked at him and said, "My name is Hither," and gave him a quick kiss.

Joseph smiled.

~ ~ ~

Later, he lay on his bed and thought about the stranger. Joseph didn't know if he liked her or not, but he remembered the Oracle's words about his twin flame and thought that Hither might be his future queen. He was obsessed with the idea that the universe was giving him a sign which could help him on his journey. No-one would believe him if he said he'd seen seven warriors and they told him he would be king, so he resolved that he would find his twin flame during his journey to claim his throne. Joseph felt lost and unsure what he should do next but his heart told him he should be in the city.

A few days later, after eating lunch with circus members, Joseph went for a walk around the city. While he was walking, he bumped into a woman. She was in a hurry and what she was carrying fell on the ground. Joseph leaned over to help her retrieve her items and opened his mouth to say he was sorry. She caught his eye and he realized she was the woman he'd met at the circus a few days ago. "Sorry, my fault," he said.

Hither, grabbing her items, looked at him face nervously and said, "No, it's my fault."

"Believe me, it was my fault. My mind was far away."

"Are you following me?" she asked.

Joseph laughed. "Why would I want to follow you? "

"I don't understand you boys."

"Boys? What? What is your problem?"

"Nothing. Nothing, and goodbye. I have things to do that are more important than you".

Joseph said in a petulant tone, "So, but what about a date? I assume everything happens for a reason, and there are no coincidences. Is it yes or no?"

Hither's disappointment was clear when she turned her back to him and said, "First, you are crazy and second what a bad day it is today."

~   ~   ~

The next day the circus wasn't giving a show and Thomas invited Joseph to take a walk with him around the city because he wanted to show him something.

Thomas pointed to the castle and said, "Joseph, here is where your father lives. If the story you told me is true, you're supposed to live here one day."

"I wish that day would come soon. One day I want you to do a show in the castle in the name of the king."

"You never know."

They returned to the circus, and Joseph told him he wanted to get to know the other side of the city, Thomas told him he had to go alone because he was needed at the circus. While Joseph was walking, he smelled the aroma of delicious bread and looking around he found a small bakery. Feeling hungry, he entered the shop and asked the Baker to give him a piece of bread.

"What's your name, young man?" the Baker asked.

"My name is Joseph, sir."

"How long have you been here in the town? And don't tell me you live here because I haven't seen you before."

Joseph said between bites of the bread, "Yes, sir, you're right. I'm new to the town. I've only been here five days."

"What are your plans?"

"Well, for now, I'm with the circus."

"Are you working in the circus?"

"No, sir, I am with them temporarily," said Joseph. "I'm looking for a job, so I can settle down."

"You don't like working in the circus?"

"It's not about working. My friend Thomas has been generous to me and given me food every day and I don't want to be a burden to him anymore."

The Baker was impressed. He said, "This shows you truly respect him, and that comes from your inner-self. Like an ice bridge – from the wider picture, we think the visible side is all there is, but in fact, the invisible part is bigger than we can imagine." Then he added, "I can offer you a job if you're interested?"

Joseph, without stopping to think, said, "Okay."

The Baker laughed. "But you don't know what the job is!"

"I assume it's related to the bakery?"

The Baker laughed again. "No, young man. It isn't here; it's in my stable."

"Stable for the horses?"

"Do you want it or not?"

"No – yes," Joseph said.

"Is that yes?"

Joseph smiled and accepted the job, asking when he should start work. The Baker told him he could start that day. Quickly, he went to his friend Thomas to tell him he'd found a job and washing to start immediately. Joseph collected his things and the sword and went to the bakery. As he entered he saw Hither there. She looked grim when she noticed him.

"Dad, there's a crazy guy here," Hither said loudly.

"Who? Joseph?" said the Baker. "Offer him some tea while I finish what I'm doing."

Joseph said while making a funny expression on his face: "You listen to him."

"Dad! What if I refuse?" Hither said.

"I don't know what your problem is," said the Baker. "You've not even met him yet."

Hither said: "Dad, it isn't that I don't want to make tea, but I don't to make tea for *him*".

Joseph said in a low voice to Hither, "If you don't make me tea, I'll tell him you sneaked into the show a few days ago."

"What did you say?" asked the Baker.

"Nothing," said Hither as she went to make tea for Joseph.

The Baker turned to Joseph and asked, "Do you have a place to sleep?" When Joseph said he didn't, the baker offered him a small room in the stable which he accepted. Hither returned with the tea for Joseph and the Baker ordered his daughter to walk with him to the stable located in their backyard. Hither showed Joseph to his room and told him, "Well, this is your room. Don't thank me and we aren't friends. Bye."

After a rest, Joseph looked around the stable. A particular horse caught his attention, and he felt compelled to go closer to him and put his hand on his chest. The Baker appeared and said, "The horse likes you. Ancient people said that a knight's horse knows the knight who will mount him."

Joseph gazed at that horse and felt a connection with it. He didn't know precisely what it was, but he imagined that he was a king while riding that horse.

The Baker saw Joseph's eyes on the horse and said, "One day, this horse will be yours." Then he left.

~ ~ ~

It was almost nightfall when Joseph went to his cozy room in the stable, putting his leather bag aside and sitting in his bed. The bottle that the Oracle had given him fell out and he grabbed it, thinking about what would happen if he drank it. *Would it help him achieve his destiny? Should he trust that woman? What about his friend's warning?* These questions filled Joseph's mind until midnight. Finally, he drank the contents of the bottle. After thirty minutes, the hallucinations hit him. The first thing that happened to him he sees his surroundings with many colors. These vivid delusions amazed him. Then everything changed. His fear swept over him as he recognized his own shadow emerging from the darkness.

Joseph panicked as a whisper called his name. He thought about his best friend Albert, their life together, and his dreams. He tried to regain control of his reactions and mind. Then he remembered the bracelet that Mariam had given him when he'd started his journey and touched it. Joseph felt as if he were in a storm in the middle of the ocean without a lifejacket. He felt that he was on an emotional rollercoaster and his emotions were fighting each other. He was scared. *Am I alive? Am I dead – or dying?*

It was hard to differentiate between the real and the unreal. Joseph he saw himself in the middle of the lake, sinking. He saw a hand and grabbed it, lifting himself out of the water. When he left the lake, he thought it was over.

But the illusions returned, over and over again.

He was hyperventilating and his pulse beat rapidly. Joseph remembered the Oracle saying that something would happen to him and he needed to face it alone. Then, he saw the Oracle in front of him. His mind flashed back to the day that the circus had celebrated his welcome. But now the circus members had become monstrous, wolf-like in nature; it seemed they wanted to chase him and feast on him – he had to run because they were seeking him as prey.

Joseph was scared and wanted this experience to end, this shift between his conscious and unconscious mind that he couldn't control.

Then he imagined he was in a long dark corridor. He walked along this corridor and saw ten rooms. To enter the final room, he needed to enter the rooms one by one. He opened the first door and saw memories of when he was young with his family. In each room he entered, were his memories of the good and the bad. The closer he got to the tenth room, the more intense his memories became, stronger and darker. He could see everything he'd done in the seventh-room. He became stuck as he felt barred from the eighth room, as there he would have to confront his traumas. And he recalled a period of his life that he had forgotten about, as if his mind had blocked specific events in his life in his best interest. He struggled with his feelings in that room as he recalled bad events and recognized his own shadow. Only three doors remained before he could end his ordeal but he couldn't reach the next one.

Then he saw the sword. It sparked and vibrates from where it was under his bed and he thought he was hallucinating again. Seven warriors circled him while with their swords on the ground before them.

"Please help me!" Joseph said.

"You don't need our help. You need to help yourself and face your fears," said one of the warriors.

"How can I face my fears? Please help me."

"To face your fears you must acknowledge them. Don't run away from them. The more you deny them, the stronger they become."

"But I'm not running from them. I'm here!"

"These rooms represent your life," said the warrior. "And what is happening is that your mind has denied bad events in your life. You can't go to the next door until you shine light on these events. Your mind thinks it's doing you a favor by blocking bad things, but to do that, it needs to block both bad and good events."

Joseph panicked and put his hands over his face as he fell to the ground. "I can't, I can't, I can't. Please help me."

"If we help you now, you will gain nothing. This loop will occur again, and again. You need to break it."

"But how?"

"You need to face it alone and allow it to be. Joseph, these are illusions your mind has created. You need to surrender and stop resisting and allow the light to enter your soul."

"But I'm resisting nothing right now!"

"Watch yourself," said the warrior, "and you will know. Listen to your thoughts and you will understand. Your mind created this experience." Then the warrior disappeared.

Joseph thought about what the warrior had said while he was feeling suffocated by his feelings and couldn't enter the eighth room. He regained control of his breath and remembered all the good things in his life. Joseph was responding to every thought that came to his mind as if it were real; this was his reality. His mind had been resisting his thoughts by denying them because the experience was a nightmare for him.

Joseph progressed to where he felt he might die and he thought, *What is the point in resisting my fear? Why not surrender? Why deny my mind?* After pondering these questions, he let go of everything in his life. A shift of energy occurred, he felt calmer, and his resistance faded second by second.

Gradually, he imagined himself leaving the seventh room and opening the door to the eighth. He felt an enormous amount of energy leave his body and he then opened the ninth door and entered the last room. Here, he saw the day he'd said goodbye to his family and he finally gained control of his mind. Joseph had entered an exquisite paradise and could see the seven warriors' faces expressing their pride.

He saw the horse in the stable waiting for him to ride. As he gazed at the bracelet on his wrist, he felt a desire to ride that horse. Joseph jumped on it horse and saw on the other side his friend Albert and all the people from his village waving to him. He rode the horse, feeling at one with nature. He felt as if his spirit had been shackled for years and now he was free, free from the shadow his mind had created for him. Joyous at his enlightenment, he felt waves of love and peace in abundance.

~ ~ ~

Joseph's family were having their afternoon tea when Mariam asked her mother, "Tell me about the night that the knights gave you Joseph. Who named him Joseph?"

"Mariam, before you were born we had our first child. He died while he was young and he was called Joseph."

Mariam was shocked. "I had a brother and he died? How? When?"

"He died eleven years before you were born and when I was giving birth to you, the midwife told me that you would be a girl. Your father came to me with a boy telling me that a knight came and gave him a boy, sword, and money to take him. I said to your father, 'God took one soul and gave us two' – you and Joseph." She started to weep and hugged Mariam, saying, "I miss Joseph."

~ ~ ~

Joseph opened his eyes and saw it was now afternoon and he was late for his first working day. He didn't want to show disrespect to the Baker who'd given him his job so he went to wash his face and quickly change his clothes. While washing, he felt for the first time that he longer carried any emotional baggage in his body or soul. Physically, Joseph felt that he'd lost a massive amount of energy, but this wasn't a physical weight. Life was giving him a second chance and now he understood how things should go and how that was part of preparing himself to achieve his destiny and claim his throne.

He dressed and went to work in the stable. Now he had begun to understand the meaning of his life and the role of the sword. Now he knew there was an invisible side to his mind that he'd been unaware of. *Why am I now aware when I wasn't before? Am I he aware enough of myself now or not?*

When Hither arrived, he didn't want to make her angry, so he greeted her warmly. However, with his new perspective, he could see that Hither wasn't mad because of him.

"How is your day going, Hither?" he asked.

"Awful! Thanks for asking."

"If you want to talk, I'm a good listener."

"And now you care, Joseph?"

"Believe me, I said nothing, and again if you want to talk, I'll listen to you until you fall asleep."

She thought for a moment and said, "Okay, but no judgment?"

Joseph smiled. "No judgment."

Hither said, "A few years ago when I was much younger, my father trusted me to go on a one week trip with my friends and when I got back home – I don't know if I want to share this."

"Hither! If you don't want to share, that's okay. But if it's something sad you need to be aware of it and not deny it!"

"When I got back, I couldn't see my mother because she had an illness that meant she needed to be isolated and –" Hither stopped suddenly.

"And what?"

"I couldn't hug her before she died because we needed to talk at a distance. I hate myself because if I hadn't gone on that trip I might have been able to hug her before she passed away."

"I'm sorry to hear that, but why take the blame for something you can't control?"

"It's my fault."

"Let's pretend that something had happened which made you cancel your trip," Joseph said. "What could you have done to stop your mother getting sick? Claiming blame might make your father suffer twice, and you don't want that. Do you?"

"No, but –"

"I think we can end your suffering right here, right now. Do you trust me?"

"I want to trust you because I don't have any choice," said Hither.

"Close your eyes."

"Is this a game?"

"You need to trust me in this. No matter how painful it is, you need to be strong. It wasn't your fault that your mother died and it's okay to have negative energy, but what isn't okay is to keep that energy in your body." Joseph paused before saying, "Imagine your mother's presence. Do you think she would be okay seeing you to take the blame for her death? This isn't your fault, and you should not grieve over events you can't control."

Hither thought about this question. Joseph asked her to close her eyes and to recall the moment when her father had told her she couldn't see her mother because of her illness. Joseph saw Hither's expression change to a sad one and assured her that she needed to feel the pain that had caused her to suffer that day.

Hither closed her eyes and said, "I'm not sure if I want to continue. I've started to feel angry."

"Hither, trust me. You only need to feel your pain that that day caused."

"It's too painful. I can see my mother in the distance, waving."

"What else do you see? Can you see her eyes?"

"It's too hazy!"

"You need to be brave to see that moment with your mind's eye and accept that the event happened in the past."

Joseph saw that she wanted to remove herself from the situation and didn't want to feel her grief. Again, he assured her she needed to feel her grief and accept it. It was hard for a few minutes, but then she cried. Joseph tried to avoid eye contact with Hither and tried to not show by any gestures that he felt empathy with her. He let her express the grief she'd kept within since her mother had died. Then, he felt a shift of energy.

Hither smiled and thanked him for listening to her story without judgment. "Joseph, what have you done for me? I haven't felt like this since the last trip I went on with my friend."

Joseph smiled and said, "Believe me, I did nothing for you. You did it for yourself."

"You did something that no-one had done for me. You helped me let go of something I had been struggling with for years."

"I did only one thing – I allowed you to express yourself without judgment."

~ ~ ~

Later, a customer came into the bakery, a soldier from the castle who wanted to order bread for the next week when the King had planned a reception because other kings were visiting. They needed a vast amount of bread for their guests to show their hospitality. Joseph asked the Baker if he could give Hither a hand delivering the bread to the castle.

The Baker said, "They want someone to deliver the bread and stay until night to help serve the guests – they are short-staffed. You'd need to stay wide awake because the King doesn't want any mistakes or his guests to be embarrassed."

"I can learn!" said Joseph.

"I can train him how to serve the bread," said Hither. "It would give me a chance to repay a favor he did for me."

"If Hither will help you, I'm okay with that," said the baker.

The Baker asked Hither to leave so he could speak privately with Joseph. He wanted to thank him for what he'd done for his daughter, helping her to let go. He told Joseph that he'd tried everything he could to help Hither see the light, but he couldn't find the best approach. The Baker put his hand on Joseph's shoulder and told him, "Joseph, the first time you entered my bakery I saw a man with a desire that was vibrating from his soul. Right away, I knew you would had a great destiny because desire is the fuel to manifest reality. No-one can conquer a man with desire because a man with desire can conquer anything."

Joseph said gratefully, "Sir, I appreciate your words and I'm grateful I had the chance to meet you. I hope that one day I can pay it forward."

"Well, young man, I don't know what you're up to but I say to you to not look at yesterday but and always look to the future. Forgive me, I'm an old man and I would like to give you some advice that I just became aware of. 'If you think there's good in life, you will receive good and if you think there is evil in life that is what you will have.' I hope you will reflect on these words because it will open your perspective for a whole new horizon, but for now I must rest."

THE MALICIOUS ADVISER

The King was eating breakfast with Princess Isabella, the daughter of his first wife Queen Amelia and Prince David, the son of the current Queen, when the his adviser, the Good Adviser, came up to him.

"Good morning, Your Majesty."

"Good morning, how are the preparations going?"

"Everything is going well, Your Majesty. The staff has been prepared since last week."

"I don't want any mistakes, do you understand?" said the King.

"Everything will be magnificent, Your Majesty."

After breakfast Prince, David went to his office and asked the guard to send in his adviser, the Bad Adviser, to talk with him about an important matter.

David's adviser arrived and greeted him. "Good morning, Your Highness."

David nodded in acknowledgement. "Tonight, the King will host a reception that all the politicians, artists, and royals will attend. We need to show that the King is of good health."

"Your Highness, I'm worried people will realize the King is sick if he gives a speech."

"That's why we need keep him at a distance from people. He can greet people by waving from the balcony. That should prevent questions."

The Bad Adviser wanted to be become the King's adviser in the future so he was willing to help Prince David become king. He was the only member of staff who had direct contact with the Prince and had taught the Prince when he was a child. Back then, the Bad Adviser had been a student of the King's adviser – who was usually called the Professor.

The Bad Adviser said to Prince David, "Your Highness, I want to tell you something important. I must share this with you if you want to be king."

"What?"

The Bad Adviser: "As you know, Your Highness, every transition in any political system around the world needs to procedures and to follow protocol we can't break."

"You're trying to teach me protocol, Adviser? You forget I was I born and raised with protocol."

"Of course not, Your Highness, but I want to share with you something the Professor taught me. Just because you're the King's son, that doesn't mean you will be the next king!"

"I don't understand. I'm the King's only son and that means I *will* be the next king."

"Your Highness, for centuries this kingdom has had traditions no-one can violate such as the sword."

"What sword?"

"You must hold the sword at your coronation and all of the Royal Council needs to show their support in the main hall as they did for your like your ancestors."

"Why has no-one told me about this?" asked David.

"I intended to but was waiting for the right moment."

"So how do I find the sword?"

"I believe it's in your father's closet because it is a precious sword because it represents the oath every king should make. He keeps it safe – but the main thing now is that your father doesn't make a speech in the main hall."

David dismissed the Bad Adviser, and thought about the sword and the throne. He'd thought he would claim the throne directly after his father's death, but he hadn't realized about these protocols.

Princess Isabella arrived and asked, "How are preparations for the ceremony going?"

"That's what I wanted to talk to you about!" said David.

"I don't think it would be a good idea for our father to give a speech today considering his bad health," Isabella said. "It would make us look weak."

"That's the last thing we want! We don't want the other kingdoms to realize the King is sick!"

"I need to do something, and I know who will help us!"

"The Professor?"

"If not him, then who?" asked Isabella. Princess Isabella was logical and independent and she cared deeply for her father. She assured David she would try her hardest to stop the King from giving a speech in the main hall.

David went to the library to see the Good Adviser and talk to him about the sword.

"Oh! Your Highness, the future king," he said.

"Future king – I'll take that as a compliment." David laughed. "I came to ask you a question, Professor."

"Please ask me anything because I'm here to serve Your Highness".

"I want to ask you about the sword that I need to become the future king. Can you tell me about it?"

"Of course, Your Highness. I never thought that one day I'd be sharing this information with you. The last time I did was when your grandfather asked me to share the story with your father."

Then the Professor began to tell David about the relationship between the kingdom and the sword. "A book called *The Testament of Flame* mentions that several centuries ago in this kingdom there had been a war for seven years. A curse they called *Scorcharis Demoaris* was spread in the world by Emperor Zaros Lobo who lived in a distant nation. Hundreds of thousands had died from starvation, war and poverty until seven warriors came together to end the tragedy by uniting the people under one banner, under one king.

"The world was in chaos and people had no-one to lead them to safety. A man called Master Goran went to the seven warriors and told them that this kingdom needed to choose a new king since the curse had killed all the royal family. He asked them to put their swords together at the zenith of the mountain when the sky started to darken. They needed to sacrifice themselves and let the spirits choose a single warrior who would take the throne for himself and his descendants.

"The warriors pledged their allegiance by taking an oath that every future king should pass this sword to the next king, telling him about the special power of the sword to help each future king to claim his throne by saying, 'This sword will find, prepare, and guide the future king to claim his rightful inheritance.'"

~ ~ ~

When Joseph had finished his work in the stable, he went to the bakery to help prepare and deliver the King's order. Joseph entered the bakery and greeted everyone, noting that the Baker was serving a customer. Someone entered the bakery and greeted the Baker who called Joseph over to them.

"Let me introduce you to Joseph," said the Baker. "He's new in town and is working with me. He's a talented young man who will make something of himself in the future."

"That is a huge compliment, sir," Joseph said shyly.

"Joseph, this is the Judge," said the Baker. "We've been friends for fifty years."

"It's a pleasure to meet you, Your Honor." said Joseph.

"Now I've made my order, please excuse me," said the Judge. "I need to go to home before I return to the courthouse."

"Joseph, how are the preparations for the King's order going?" asked the Baker. "Are you ready to deliver the bread to the castle and spend the night there serving the King's guests?"

"Everything's ready, and I'm ready to deliver the order."

"Good! Now you need to set off in the caravan and get to the castle early."

~ ~ ~

While the staff were making the arrangements for the King's reception, Isabella was double-checking everything. She noticed the Good Adviser and said, "Hello, Professor. How is everything going?"

"Excellently! Although it's unorthodox for you to drop by and check everything yourself, isn't it?"

Isabella laughed.

"Isabella, I've known you since you were young," the King's Adviser continued, "and I know things about you that you don't know about yourself." Then he laughed and asked what she wanted.

"I dropped by to tell you I'm concerned about my father making a speech in the main hall," said Isabella, "because of his bad health. We don't anyone to suspect that he isn't well."

"A good observation. You've always cared more about the throne than your father, which makes me proud of you. Thanks for sharing your concerns. I'll keep them under consideration. But now I must focus on my work and you need to get ready for tonight."

~ ~ ~

Joseph arrived at the castle in amazement because he'd never thought he'd enter the castle. He said to the guard, "Hello, sir. I'm the bread contractor and I'm here for the King's reception. Would you mind guiding me where should I go? It's a massive castle and I might get lost."

"You're right on time!" the guard said. "Let me escort you to Mr. Jean-Pascal LaRue."

"Who is he?"

"He's second-in-command when it comes to following protocol. My advice is to never make a mistake. He's a perfectionist."

Joseph followed the guard to where Mr. LaRue was greeting the staff and giving them the instructions they needed to follow while working at the King's reception.

"Hello everybody," said Mr. LaRue. "I believe you all know why you're here. Let me introduce myself, I am the assistant for protocol in this castle and am responsible for every event the King holds in the castle. I know the number of staff, rooms, spoons, supplies – everything down to how many ants there are in this castle – so don't to bend the rules because, believe me, I will know. And when I will know, you won't like it. I accept only perfection and will not settle for less. Now go about your work."

Then he turned to Joseph and said, "Hey! You, young man. Why are you dressed like that? Haven't you realized you'll be serving at the King's reception?"

"I beg your pardon, sir. This is the first time I've served the King."

"Who are you?"

"Joseph, sir. The Baker sent me."

"The Baker? Usually he sends his daughter."

"I'm his new worker, sir."

Mr. LaRue called loudly to one of the castle maids, "Demeter!"

"Yes, Mr. LaRue?"

"Please make sure that this young man is well-dressed well for tonight. What's your name again?"

"Joseph, sir."

Demeter took Joseph away and gave him an outfit to wear.

~   ~   ~

Dark was beginning to fall as the guests arrived. The staff stood in a row to greet them. When most of the guests had arrived, the royal guards blew their trumpets to announce the King's arrival. One of the guards said loudly, "Please stand up to welcome our king."

The King appeared at the top of the banquet table and waved as his guests stood to show their respect to him. A second trumpet sounded a welcome to Princess Isabella. She appeared from the stairs dressed so lavishly and elegantly that the guests could hardly bear to look at her. A third trumpet welcomed Prince David who was wearing formal royal dress and had his adviser walking behind him.

Isabella and David greeted and shook hands with the guests, while the staff served royal delights – tiny bites of caviar, salmon, sweetmeats... Joseph was shocked because he saw his siblings in and wondered if he dared speak to them. In the end, he decided not to and got on with serving the guests with bread.

Isabella was speaking to one of the guests. "Yes, Your Excellency. I can assure you that our kingdom will work with yours to resolve our problems. I'll tell the King personally about your concerns."

"Your Highness, you have proved to me that the King is your father. You are just like him."

"I take that as a compliment, Your Excellency. Let me offer you some of the most delicious bread in our kingdom." She pointed to Joseph.

Joseph walked over to Isabella. He bowed and served the bread to her and her guest. His mind drifted as he looked at Isabella's face and she noticed and made eye contact with him.

"Do I know you?" asked Isabella. "Your face seems familiar."

Time stood still for Joseph and Isabella. Isabella had a feeling of déjà vu as she looked into Joseph's eyes, a strange feeling as if she knew him. She had to remind herself that he was a servant and she needed to continue her conversation with the guest.

Joseph had mixed feelings. He was happy to see his sister for the first time but sad because she didn't know he was her brother. He had to keep control of his emotions and focus on his task. "No, Your Highness," he said. "I'm only the bread server and this is my first time here."

Joseph went to another guest to serve bread but Isabella continued to gaze at him and she lost track of the conversation she'd been having with the guest.

"Pardon me, Your Highness?" said the guest.

"Nothing, sorry," said Isabella. "I was distracted for a moment. I'll deliver your message to the King." She went to greet another guest but was overcome with the feeling that there was a mysterious connection between her and the bread servant – but she didn't know what it was. She put the idea aside and focused on greeting more guests.

~ ~ ~

Because of the discussion David had had with his adviser that afternoon, he'd gone to his father's room and searched in his closet for the sword, knowing that no-one would notice his absence, but he couldn't find anything. He couldn't ask anyone to help him search for the sword because they all believed that the sword was with the King in a safe place. David looked everywhere in his father's room, opening the closets and boxes that his father kept his valuables in, but he couldn't find anything. He decided to find his adviser.

David returned to the main hall, nervously looking around for his adviser and ignoring everyone who greeted him. Joseph offered him some bread but David ignored him. When David was near Joseph, he heard Isabella her say to a guest, "Let me search for my brother David. I'm sure he'll help you with this matter."

Isabella turned and saw David. "David! David! Would you mind coming over here? It's urgent!" David ignored her.

Isabella said to the guest, "Sorry about that. It seems David is busy, but I can assure you that I will speak to him soon."

David saw his adviser and called out, "Where have you been? Now! Follow me! It's urgent!"

The bread Joseph had was finished, so he asked one of his colleagues where the main kitchen was so he could get more. David and the Bad Adviser had gone into a room to talk and his Adviser had forgotten to close the door. While Joseph was searching for the kitchen, he heard the word "sword" from the room next to him. He pricked up his ears.

"I couldn't find the sword, it's disappeared!" David said,

"How has it disappeared, Your Highness?" asked the Bad Adviser:

"I told you," said David angrily. "I went to my father's room, and searched everywhere and I couldn't find the sword."

"Your Highness, this is a major problem because without it there's is a possibility you might not become king."

David raised his voice. "You're my Adviser and you need to help me. Do you want to be the king's Adviser? Find a solution."

The Bad Adviser thought for a moment, and wanted to lure David by addressing him with 'your majesty' instead of 'your Highness' to feed David's ego by saying: "Your Highness, sorry, Your Majesty to be, there is a solution, but we need to work together and you need to assure me I will be your only adviser when you become King."

"Deal. Tell me what you have."

"Your Highness, the sword and the ceremony act as a form of protocol to lead to the legal king, and it was created to find attunement between the King and the Royal Council in front of the people. If the King indirectly supports you in front of them, and they agree that you should be king, maybe we can use that in the future. We need the King to support you in front of everyone.

But we don't want him to give a speech in case that suggests he isn't capable of making decisions."

"So what do you suggest?"

"I know you've agreed with your sister and the King's Adviser that the King won't make a speech tonight, but we need him to endorse the future king." He paused. "I have an idea!"

"What is it?"

"Since all the members of the Royal Council are attending the ceremony maybe an endorsement from your father, the King, mentioning the exact words the 'future king' would be helpful."

"But his word alone won't make me king. And the Royal Council knows that."

"Your Majesty, even if the King didn't intend to say it in that way, it would remove any potential doubt in the future. You're our future king and you need to claim your rightful inheritance. You're Edmund's son and therefore our future king. I can see only one obstacle – the King's Adviser!"

"The Professor?"

"He is an obstacle, Your Highness!"

"Don't harm him! We don't want blood."

"But the ends justify the means."

"I told you, don't kill the Professor."

The Bad Adviser: "Your Majesty, it's important to prepare a speech before everyone is dismissed, a speech in which your father says the words 'future king'."

Joseph was still listening and his heartbeat started to increase and his feet were frozen to the ground because he was so shocked about what he had just listened to. He continued on toward the kitchen to get the bread while his mind was fixed on the conspiracy that his half-brother and the Bad Adviser wanted to fabricate to manipulate the King so David could take the throne.

~ ~ ~

David took a small piece of paper and wrote a speech saying that the King welcomed his guests and was proud to have his son help him to run his kingdom. David intentionally referred to himself as the future king to build his case for when he would confront the Royal Council after his father's death. He then went to his father and convinced him to give the speech without telling Isabella or the Professor. The King finally agreed.

The guards blew their trumpets to announce that the King was about to speak which drew the close attention of both Isabella and the Professor.

"First, I want to welcome you," began the King. "Second, I hope you will all enjoy my reception. I want to thank everyone who has been involved in organizing this event. Finally, I want to announce that my son, your future king, will be married soon"

Everyone applauded at this happy news, while Isabella was shocked by what she'd heard. *David was to marry soon?* He hadn't even said he was in love with anyone. It seemed he would say anything that could make his father address him as the "future king."

While the guests expressed their happiness about what they had just heard to David, Isabella pulled him aside and said, "I don't understand you, David? How? And when? Who's the lucky woman you will marry?"

David said nervously, "I can't tell you because she doesn't want anyone to know her identity."

"A secret lover! I never thought that one day a girl would fall in love with you."

"The main reason I want to be married," said David, "is that I want my father to see his grandson before he dies."

Isabella shook her head in disbelief.

~ ~ ~

At the end of the evening, everyone was dismissed, allowing the staff to clean up. Joseph thought about the conspiracy between his half-brother and the Bad Adviser. He didn't know what he should do because he thought that no-one would believe him.

He returned to the bakery to give the Baker his payment for his bread and the services he'd supplied. After he'd gone to his bed in the stable, he lay down, thinking about everything that had happened that day from seeing his sister Isabella, his father the King, and his half-brother David.

Joseph was wounded by the idea that his half-brother would betray their father because he wanted to become king, so he cleared his mind and went for a walk in the middle of the night while everyone was sleeping. Suddenly, Joseph saw a young man sitting in the street and he looked starving and cold. Joseph felt sorry for him so he drew closer.

"Good evening. What are you doing here at this time? Do you want any help?"

The stranger said, "I'm waiting for the Professor to bring me food, but today he didn't come – for the first time."

"Who's the Professor?"

"For months a man who calls himself the Professor has helped me. He's generous and if he couldn't come himself, he sent someone. Now, I'm starving."

"Come with me!" said Joseph.

Joseph looked into his eyes and then asked him to come with him. They went to the bakery and Joseph gave him some food and went to his room and took a third of his money to give the young man. Joseph had spent a third on the Oracle and had now given a third away, leaving only a third of his money. He was happy to sacrifice his need for others because he knew he didn't need that money since he slept and ate in the Baker's house and that cost him nothing. "Take this money and the bread," he said.

"Thank you, but this is a lot and I can't accept it from you, sir."

"I didn't earn it. My foster father gave it to me when I started my journey. How come you're in this position?"

"I have a debt that I need to pay and I don't have any job because of it. I used to be a guard in the prison, forty-two miles from the city. One day, the chief officer in the prison accused me of stealing some money I was in charge of. He said he would do me a favor and not to send me to the disciplinary court because I had been a loyal guard since my first day. He ended my job for a while till I could save the same amount of money and repay the debt. He knows that to earn that amount of money will take me at least five years of hard work but with your money I can return my job."

The young man thanked Joseph and said that one day he would return the favor. Joseph told him he shouldn't thank him because something had inspired him to leave his bed and have a walk, and then he saw him and felt it was right is to give him food and money. Joseph said goodbye and returned to his room and slept peacefully.

MANAGED CHAOS

Joseph woke up early and went about his daily routine. After he had finished his work, he went to the bakery to see if he could offer any help to the Baker. The Baker was arguing with the Wheat Supplier because he wanted to increase the price of a bushel of wheat and that meant the Baker would lose a lot of money because he couldn't cover his cost of the new price of wheat. Joseph remained silent as he listened to their conversation. Finally, he interrupted them. "Sir, you want to increase the price of a bushel of wheat, is that correct?"

"Yes, young man," the Wheat Supplier said. "The Baker can't understand why I need to increase my prices but the place where I get my supply has been vandalized so I need to set a new price."

"How much did you used to sell one bushel of wheat to the Baker for?"

"I used to sell it for one coin. Now, I need to sell it for one and a half coins per bushel to cover my costs."

"How many bushels can you put in this caravan, and how many bushels have you delivered today?"

"I can carry two hundred bushels in this caravan," the Supplier said, "but the Baker only needs a hundred bushels each week."

Joseph told him that if he maximized the space in his caravan with two hundred bushels, and only delivered to the Baker every two weeks, he could offer his loyal customers a better price because he had already paid the cost of rental for the caravan and only had to do one delivery every two weeks. If he did the math, he would discover that he had covered his costs and made a profit without increasing his sale price. The Supplier mused for a moment and said: "Brilliant idea, young man."

The Baker was impressed that Joseph had fixed the problem. Joseph and the Baker went back inside the bakery to see that the Judge was there and had a young pretty girl with him. They said hello and Joseph couldn't take his eyes off the girl.

The Judge said, "Let me introduce you to my little angel, Karma."

Joseph remembered what the Oracle had told him about meeting his twin flame. He thought that she might be his future queen. The Judge spent only a few minutes in the bakery – Joseph wanted to do anything he could to make them stay longer. As the Judge and Karma were leaving the bakery, Joseph called out. "Karma, wait a second."

"Yes, Joseph?"

"I'm grateful that your father has introduced us and was wondering if you'd like to take a walk with me one day."

Karma said shyly, "I'd like to because you're new to the town and my father told me you're a good young man."

Joseph couldn't believe what had just happened, and he jumped for joy.

The Judge said, "Well, young man, don't you have a job to do?"

"Your Honor," Joseph responded, "you are an amazing father and you have a lovely little angel." And he bowed.

Karma said, "See you next week at the same time."

~ ~ ~

Joseph entered the bakery, his face full of happiness. Then the baker asked him, "Do I see someone who has found his twin flame?"

"What?"

"Young man, you're in love; I can see it in your eyes."

Joseph felt nervous and tried to control his expression. "Who? Me? I don't think so, sir."

"As you wish, young man, but let me give you a piece of advice about love. If Karma is your twin flame, you needn't impress her, compliment her or even buy any gifts because what is meant to be is inevitable."

~ ~ ~

Back in the castle, Isabella said to David, "Have you seen the Professor? It's the afternoon and I haven't seen him today."

"Nor me," said David, "but he told me that he has to go to another kingdom on a business matter."

"I was with him throughout the reception and he didn't mention that to me."

"You know him, Isabella. He's getting old and forgetful."

"Maybe," said Isabella as she left.

David requested that the Bad Adviser to come to talk with him. When he arrived, David said, "Isabella asked me where the Adviser was and I lied to her. Do you know where he is?"

The Bad Adviser said, "Your Highness, if I tell you now, you might get angry, but if you want to be the future king, you need to follow my plan." And then he bowed.

"You need to tell me now," said David.

"I sent the Professor to the prison."

"We didn't agree that we would send the Professor to prison," said David angrily. "I didn't order you to do that."

"Your Highness, getting rid of the Professor will eliminate many things in the future that would prevent us from making you our future king."

"But everyone will notice!"

The Bad Adviser edged closer to David and said, "Your Highness, I taught you everything I knew when your father assigned me as your tutor, and I will be at your side until I die. I know that you're the rightful king."

"I'm not sure this is a good idea."

"Don't you want to be king, with everyone kneeling before you, and asking for your approval and mercy?" asked the Bad Adviser. "Your father has become forgetful and he might forget to mention to the Royal Council that you will be the future king."

David was imagining himself as king. When the Bad Adviser saw David's eyes fill with conceit, he told David that he needed to become king as soon as possible because before long people would notice the absence of the Professor and become suspicious. The Bad Adviser didn't explicitly say what needed to happen next because he didn't think David was ready – they needed to get rid of David's father. The Bad Adviser decided to keep feeding David's ego, to keep pushing the idea that he would be king so he would eventually agree to get rid of his father.

~ ~ ~

Back at the stable, Joseph was cleaning when Hither came to greet him. She said, "A little bird told me that someone is falling in love? Is it true?"

Joseph feeling embarrassed: "What? Who told you that? I don't want to be in love. I'm too young for love."

"Too young to love? Seriously?"

Joseph responded by pulling a face. "Could you imagine me in love?"

"Karma is a pretty woman, and I have known her since I was young," said Hither, "but do you truly have feelings for her?"

"Maybe."

"Maybe? You can't say that, Joseph!"

"She is very beautiful."

"Just because she's beautiful, that doesn't mean that you love her, Joseph."

Joseph wasn't sure if he loved her or not because he rationalized that he must love her and that she was his twin flame, his future queen because that was what the Oracle had told him. He felt a euphoric rush when he saw her but wasn't sure if he loved her or simply liked her.

At that moment, the baker called out. "Joseph, there's someone here who wants to talk to you."

Joseph went into the bakery and saw the guy to whom he'd given a third of his money. He was in a guard's uniform.

"Wow," said Joseph, "I see that you got your job back!"

"Yes, because you gave me a third of your money and I've come to thank you. You did something that I won't forget for the rest of my life."

"I didn't need it. That day I'd felt anxious so I took a walk and I saw you. It's a coincidence, believe me."

"What coincidences make you come to me in the night? The man who called himself the Professor didn't come to me that night. For months he'd come to me during the night to give me food, but that night he didn't come, and you showed up instead of him."

"I don't know your name, Guard."

"You're a good man, Joseph, for giving me your money without knowing my name," said the stranger. "My name is Richard and I am in your debt."

"Thank you for your kind words," Joseph responded. "It's nice to know you, Richard, and I'm happy that you got your job back. I don't think I'll ever need a favor from someone who works in a prison, but thanks."

"You never know, Joseph."

~ ~ ~

A week later Joseph was getting ready to meet Karma, practicing what he would say when she arrived. *I am so happy to have a walk with you, Karma; It's a pleasure to meet you, Karma, thank you for giving me your time.*

Eventually, Karma arrived at the bakery wearing a purple dress that made Joseph's heart to beat faster. From the moment she entered the bakery, Joseph couldn't take his eyes off her; she was a little angel.

Karma planned to take him to a secret spot that few people knew, telling him that she liked to go there when she wanted to hide from life. Joseph thought about his friend Albert and how they liked to go to similar places. This made Joseph like Karma more because they had something in common.

When they arrived, Joseph said, "This lake is lovely, and I admire your choice."

"Thanks, Joseph. That's nice of you to say."

"It reminds me of my friend Albert, and how we like to go to similar places."

Karma responded, "So, Joseph, why do you want to go out with me?"

"I see that you're a good person, Karma."

"Well, thank you, Joseph, and I see that in you."

Joseph said: "Karma, I want to say something to you, that…"

"That what?"

Joseph said shyly, "I think I have feelings for you but I'm not sure what they are it. I know it sounds crazy and it isn't right to be so unsure, but… I don't know. I felt that I needed to share that with you."

Then they talked for hours. Minute by minute, Joseph became more certain that Karma was his twin flame and therefore, his future queen. He felt a connection, and there was no reason not to be a king and a queen to fulfill his destiny. Joseph couldn't take his eyes off Karma and thought, *Is she my future queen? We have clicked, and there is no reason to believe that Karma is not my twin flame!*

~ ~ ~

The Bad Adviser was putting the finishing touches on his plan to meet with David to empower him to be king. He said, "Your Highness, now it's time to become king!"

"How? What do you mean? How can I take the throne if my father is still alive?"

"You know what we should do."

"Are you suggesting that I should kill my father?" David asked.

"Your Highness, your father has served his kingdom well for the last thirty years. Now it is time for him to pass the throne to his only son."

David was unconvinced but the Bad Adviser started to tempt him with thoughts about what it would mean to be king. "I fear something," said the Bad Adviser, "which is that maybe your father gave the sword to your sister Isabella so she would be the first queen of the kingdom. You know how many times your father has assigned her with the kingdom's management."

As soon as David heard that, he believed that it might be true, that his sister might become Queen. For a moment, David started to rationalize that he needed to get rid of his father not because he wanted to become king but because he would be the best person to run the kingdom. He said, "Let's move on, Adviser, but I can't do it, you need to do it."

"As you wish, Your Majesty, but before that, we need to do something that is vital if you are to position yourself as the future king."

"What?"

"Before we get rid of your father, and argue the case for you becoming king before front of the Royal Council, we need to show them that you can handle any problem that might face your kingdom."

The Adviser told him that the last part of the plan was to create chaos that no one could stop except them. The idea was to bribe a few groups in the kingdom and have them vandalize property, creating conflict between citizens. At the same time, they could position David as king and the people would endorse him. The King's words at the reception would be an endorsement that no one would doubt. This would show the Royal Council that sometimes the transition in any political system might change from era to era, and they should do with whatever the kingdom might need.

Once the Bad Adviser had received David's approval, he went to the city with his guards to meet criminals he knew to arrange what they should do in the next few days.

The Bad Adviser talked to a gang leader saying, "Hey Jimmy. It's been a long time!"

"What do I owe you this time?"

The Bad Adviser threw him a big bag filled with money. "Take this. I need you to do something urgent – and don't talk to the King's Adviser in that way because one day you will need him."

The Bad Adviser described the plan of creating chaos in the kingdom in such a way that it would look like the kingdom might collapse. He assured the gang leader that no-one would arrest him. The gang leader saw an opportunity bigger than the money that the Bad Adviser gave him, so he said he needed more than money. He wanted protection from him and the future king so no other gang leader could enter his territory. The Bad Adviser looked him up and down and agreed to his demand.

~ ~ ~

After Joseph and Karma had chatted, Joseph dropped her back at the Judge's house. Joseph returned to the stable and while in bed he thought obsessively about every second he'd spent with Karma. He could remember every conversation, her body language and facial expressions. Then, he realized he'd spent hours thinking about her. And he thought about talking to Hither about whether he loved her or liked her. It was possible that he didn't love her, Maybe his liking was an attachment that his mind had created based on the influence of the Oracle's words.

The next morning, Joseph woke to the sound of people screaming. He jumped from his bed and ran to the bakery – it was in total disarray. Sacks of flour were burst open and scattered everywhere. Trays had been thrown around the room. He went outside and saw that almost all the market stalls near the bakery had also been vandalized and supplies had been stolen.

Joseph spoke to a woman who was staring at the damage. "What's going on?"

"We woke up to this. We don't know who did it."

Chaos had spread throughout the city. No-one considered this could be the Prince's plan. Why would the person responsible for their protection vandalize their property?

~   ~   ~

In the castle, the Bad Adviser was talking to David. "Your Highness, I feel we should proceed to the last part of the plan."

"I thought we'd done the last part!"

"We need to get rid of the King."

"You didn't say we'd need to kill my father!" said David.

"This is in your best interest. Don't you want to be king?"

"I want to be king, but not by killing my father."

Your Highness, we should always consider the possibility that your father may secretly want to make your sister Isabella queen!"

"He can't do that!" David said angrily.

"But you know how many times your father has assigned her responsibility for the kingdom's affairs."

"I will not let my sister Isabella be the Queen because I am the oldest, I am Edmund's son!"

"You are born to be the King of Zelaar."

"Yes, I am the King, I am the only king."

"Shall we proceed with our plans?"

Before he dismissed his Adviser, David said, "Please be careful. We don't want anyone to suspect that we've killed the King."

Stealthily, the Bad Adviser put poison in the King's lunch and gave it to the King to eat. After a few hours, the King started to feel sick. He had a fever, and kept vomiting, as well as complaining of a sore throat. The Bad Adviser yelled, "Someone call a doctor right now!"

The Doctor arrived swiftly. "Good afternoon. What do we have today?"

"I don't know," said the Bad Adviser. "I came to check on the King as Prince David asked me to and I saw him like that!"

"May I check him, please?"

After a cursory examination, the Doctor said, "I think he has the flu. What is important now is that he get rest and no-one should be in contact with the King for a few days."

After three days the King died. The bells rang and the flags were lowered. Everyone was saying, "The King is dead."

The Royal Council came to offer their condolences to Isabella and David. One member of the Royal Council said, "We are sorry to hear this news. It's hard to lose someone like your father."

Isabella said sadly, "Thank you. You now have a tough decision to make about who will be the next king. We, with the rest of the kingdom, will accept the decision that the council makes."

"Thank you, Your Highness. We will do our best. And…"

"And what?"

"We know it's not an ideal time to ask this, but I was wondering if your father had mentioned anything about the sword? Like where is the sword, who is the sword holder?"

"Well, I would like to help you in this matter, but my father didn't mention where it is kept."

"I beg your pardon, Your Highness, but it's important to know who holds the sword because our decision of who is the rightful heir relies on it."

"Is it possible that your father gave the sword to you or to Prince David?"

"Not to me and I don't think he gave it to David, but it is possible. I think only one person knows the answer to your question."

"Who?"

"The Professor – but he's missing!"

The Council Member looked embarrassed as he said, "Is it possible that your father has another son alive?"

"What! I don't think so!" exclaimed Isabella.

"Sorry to take up your time, Your Highness."

The Royal Council entered into a debate about who would be the next king. They were waiting for the sword owner to appear. That was supposed to be the son of the king – in this case, David. Also they needed the help of the Professor, but no-one knew where he was. Day by day, gang activities escalated, with vandalism, killing and stealing. People were living in chaos and fear and started to kill each other for food because most of the crops were stolen.

~   ~   ~

Joseph cried all night after hearing about the King's death. He'd felt that his half-brother was planning to do something evil, but he'd been powerless to prevent it. He also felt guilty that he'd done nothing and that he couldn't say goodbye to his father and tell him that he had another living son. So many 'what if's'… But he couldn't do anything and no-one would believe his story.

Suddenly, the sword began to vibrate and spark under his bed. He grabbed it and the seven warriors appeared before him. But there was something different about them – the warrior who'd been in the middle had moved to the right and the warrior who'd been the seventh on the far left had disappeared. After focusing on the warrior in the middle, he figured out that it was his father.

The King's ghost spoke to Joseph, saying, "You didn't know me?"

"Father! How come? You have died?"

"Joseph, my boy, I'm sorry. I hadn't known that I had a living son. Your mother sacrificed you without telling me because she wanted to protect you." He looked at the warriors and said, "It seems that these warriors inspired her to send you away to be the true future king."

Joseph lowered his head. "Father, I'm sorry. I could have prevented this from happening if I'd talked to the guard about my half-brother's plan to get rid of you."

"My son, this is bigger than you and me. Even if I'd known about it, I might not have been able to stop it. This is part of the prophecy of preparing you to be the future king."

"What do you mean?"

"It is an oath that the seven warriors swore centuries ago to help and prepare the rightful candidate to become king. It is a responsibility that each of us should pass it to others."

"Does that mean I will be responsible one day?"

"Yes, my son. Every king who dies in this kingdom will transmute to be a warrior within the seven warriors to guide the rightful king."

"Do you mean that those next to you are my ancestors?"

The King pointed to the warrior on his right. "This is my father, your grandfather. On his left is my grandfather! It is your journey now to be king, and in the future you will be next to each other to guide the rightful king after you. You are the rightful king and you will save the kingdom from its current ordeal. I believe in you."

"But Father, I don't know how to do it," Joseph replied. "No-one will believe that I am the future king. No-one knows that you had another living son."

The King put his hand on Joseph's shoulder. "Joseph, my son, now you may not be king, but in the future you will be. The more you accept your call, the closer you will be to achieving your destiny."

"What is my call?"

"Your destiny is to become king and everything that has happened to you was a call. If you accept these, you will move a step closer toward your destiny. Even the first time you grabbed the sword when you were eleven years old, was a call. And when you saw the sword for the second time, it was a call."

"What will happen if I reject the call?"

"When you accept your call, you will fulfill your destiny. You could refuse the call, but you would face many consequences. These consequence might affect you and your surroundings, and sometimes your call is outwardly bad, but internally good, and vice versa."

"You said that sooner or later, I will be king?" Joseph asked.

"If you accept the call earlier, you might save the kingdom from damage, but if you refuse it your brother will take the throne.

He isn't fit to be king – under him, starvation, war, and poverty will increase. One day you will accept the call but many people will have lost their lives."

Then the seven warriors disappeared.

PROPAGANDA

At the Royal Council meeting with all the ministers and politicians, Mr. LaRue attended in place of the King's Adviser to act as Head of Protocol. They were meeting privately to discuss who would be the next king. The traditional way was to sit in a circle and the future king was supposed to hold the sword while the Royal Council showed their support. The King would then stand up with the sword while the Royal Council surrounded him till the sword sparked to indicate the ancestors' presence. Usually, the King would give the sword to the future king, but the sword was missing and the King had died before the council could speak to him about the transition. And this process had become much harder because the Professor had disappeared.

During the meeting, no one was allowed to leave and no one was allowed to enter from outside. They spent from morning until the afternoon discussing the transition, the best candidate, and the riots. David and the Bad Adviser sat outside, waiting for the council's decision, knowing that they would take longer than usual because of the situation. David wanted to enter the meeting and was refused by the guard despite being the Prince.

The guard said, "Sorry, Your Highness. I have strict orders to not let anyone enter the meeting."

"Don't you know who I am?"

"Of course, Your Highness. You are Prince David."

David pushed the door and entered and walked to the center where everyone could see him clearly. He said loudly, "Our Royal Council, who has devoted its life and time to serve this kingdom and my father. Today, you have a huge responsibility in choosing the future king and I am here to give you my support. I hope you will make your decision soon because the kingdom might fall due to the riots that began before my father died. The people of this kingdom count on your wise decision."

The speaker of the Royal Council said, "Prince David, I assure you that we will do our best to make our decision soon but we must follow procedure."

"I thank you for your loyalty to the kingdom and to my father," David said, "and I urge you to decide on the future king soon."

"Prince David, for centuries the Royal Council has followed the same process but our dilemma is that we don't know who the sword holder is because he hasn't appeared yet."

"Why not to modernize the way we elect the future king?" David asked.

"Your Highness, we agreed to follow the procedure our ancestors have followed. The sword is a significant symbol for this kingdom."

"I know that you will disagree with me, but isn't it the time for change? We need to follow what this era provides. This might be new testimony from the spirits, meaning new rules."

"Are you suggesting we should modernize our procedure?"

"Don't you remember in the last ceremony my father made a speech and specifically said the words 'my future king'?" David asked.

"Yes, Your Highness, but that endorsement doesn't mean that *you* are the future king."

"But don't you see? The sword is missing for the first time, For the sake of the kingdom, I nominate myself as King of Zelaar if I can stop the riots within three days. If I succeed, this will be a sign. It will show that I will be a good king."

The Royal Council looked at each other and began to whisper amongst themselves. Finally, a member of the Council spoke. "For centuries we have preserved the oath of the seven warriors to elect the rightful king following the same process."

Another member of the Royal Council said, "Maybe it is a sign from the spirits, the seven warriors."

Finally, the speaker of the Royal Council said, "Stop, everyone! Prince David, we will consider your offer. Please wait outside while we discuss it. You can expect our decision before the sun goes down."

~ ~ ~

David and his Adviser went to a room to talk privately. David said, "We need to make them take my offer seriously."

"What do you suggest, Your Highness?"

"Go to the gang leader and tell him to increase the intensity of the riots. We need an atrocity that the Royal Council will get to hear about!"

"Your wish is my command. I'll send a message to him."

~ ~ ~

The speaker of the Royal Council, "What is that? Can anyone else hear the screaming?"

Another member added, "What's going on? We need to send someone to find out."

A third member of the Royal Council said, "I suggest one of us goes to find out what's going on."

The speaker said, "I suggest that three of us go instead of one. This report is crucial and might change the way that we will elect the next king."

A few hours later, before the sun had gone down, the three members returned to the Royal Council. The speaker said, "The word that describes what is happening is *brutality*."

A member of the Royal Council asked, "Do you suggest accepting Prince David's offer?"

"It is up to you all! Let's vote on it. Whoever wants to accept Prince David's offer should raise his hand."

A short time later they called David and told him that they had accepted his offer.

~ ~ ~

From the early morning until the afternoon, David and his Adviser walked around the city to show their sympathy and to enhance his image with the citizens, assuring them that he would punish whoever was responsible for what had happened. David went to every shop and stall that had been vandalized, talking to the common people. He even made a speech in the middle of the city. David ordered his Adviser to offer compensation to everyone from his own money, not the kingdom's. Everyone who heard this thanked him loudly and called his name. This news began to spread throughout the city and people started to like David, believing he was a good man and would make a good king.

David said to his Adviser while mounting his horse before returning to the castle, "Do you believe they will buy it?"

"Your Highness, people are governed by two things – fear and ignorance. I suggest you start writing your coronation speech right now because you will be king. And don't forget our deal that I should be your only adviser."

"When I become king you will get everything you want. First, I need to be king."

~ ~ ~

Karma dropped by to speak with Joseph while he was in the stable. When she entered the stable, Joseph was working so she sneaked up and put her hands over Joseph's eyes before he'd realized someone was there. Joseph felt a soft hand upon his eyes and sensed it was Karma's hand. He looked around to see Karma.

"It's nice of you to drop by," Joseph said.

"I wanted to say that I enjoyed our conversation at the lake and I'd like it if we went on another trip together next week."

"I'm in, but I need to get permission from the Baker."

~ ~ ~

By the next day, the riots had increased to a point where people were feeling desperate panic. They began to steal from each other and the Royal Council was waiting fearfully to see if David could do anything to stop what was happening. The Bad Adviser suggested that David keep the situation as it was for three days more. Also, David needed to go to the city to enhance his image with citizens and assure them he would end this tragedy soon.

When David thought it was the right moment, he ordered his Adviser to go to the gang leader and tell him to stop everything immediately. The next morning, the riots ended. The Royal Council heard the news, but they decided to stay together three days more to make sure that the riots had truly ended. Within three days, all the citizens had started to call David's name, showing their support for him as their future king.

In the Royal Council, the members were debating after three days of discussion.

One member of the council said, "We are here to decide who will be fit to become our king. We have a task to perform for which history holds us accountable."

"I know this is unorthodox," said another member, "and we don't usually break with tradition, especially when it comes to the king and the sword, but it seems that this is a sign from the spirits."

Other members agreed with the previous member and one said, "It seems that the best candidate is David. I'll give him my vote. If he can handle such riots without being king, what could he do as king?"

So the Royal Council agreed that making David king was the best decision, sacrificing tradition for the greater good of the kingdom. They called David and told him that they would give him their blessing and advocate for him to be the future king.

In the afternoon, David was ready to be announced as king and dictated the speech he would make when the Royal Council officially announced him. He placed the crown on his head, thinking of the moment that he would be king.

Isabella saw him do this and said, "It seems that my brother soon will be king."

"And you are the brother of the king, and I can't wait to be the king," David replied.

"You will be. Don't rush it. By the way, how did you stop the riots?"

"I learned a lot of things from my father."

"You're definitely ready for the coronation, and now I should go to get ready myself."

~ ~ ~

When it was time for David to become king, he sat in the main hall while the members of the Royal Council, ministers, and politicians endorsed him. They conducted a private coronation due to the circumstances. David stood and thanked everyone for their dedication in the past and assured them that he would continue to need their help and advice with following the new testimony. He then swore he would punish those who'd taken part in the riots.

On the first day of David's rule as King, he called the Bad Adviser.

"Your Majesty let me use this moment to congratulate you," said the Bad Adviser.

"Thank you. Now, how should we punish the people responsible for the riots? I need to maintain my image in front of the people so what do you suggest?"

"Your Majesty, we need to arrest few people and say we have evidence that they were behind the riots, but we shouldn't arrest anyone from the gang because they might talk."

David requested the Chief of Guard to come to him. He arrived while David was sitting on his throne with his Adviser still present.

"How are you?" David said to the Chief of Guard.

"I'm feeling good, Your Majesty," General Graham responded, "and I want to congratulate you on becoming king. I promise you that I will be loyal to you no matter what you ask of me."

David glanced at the Bad Adviser and smiled. "I admire your dedication and I want to assign to you an important matter." He explained that he needed to arrest a few people so he could maintain his image in front of the public.

"I can assure you, Your Majesty, that I will open an investigation to find who was responsible for the riots."

"Don't open an investigation!" exclaimed David.

"Then how can I find who the culprits were, Your Majesty?"

The Bad Adviser intervened. "His Majesty needs to maintain his image. Don't you understand?"

"But, Your Majesty," said General Graham. "I can't arrest people for something that they didn't do."

"It seems you have forgotten that I am King, haven't you? As your King I order you to obey me."

"You heard the King, didn't you, General?" added the Bad Adviser.

"Your wish is my command, Your Majesty."

Soon after, the guards went into the city to look for anyone who was acting suspiciously so they might arrest them.

~   ~   ~

As soon as Karma arrived at the bakery, she saw the guards arresting Joseph. Hither was crying. They knew that Joseph hadn't done anything wrong. The guard told Karma that there'd be a hearing the next day and if Joseph wasn't guilty, they might pardon him.

Karma went to her father, the Judge, saying, "I went to meet Joseph and I saw the guards arresting him because they believed that he was part of the riots."

"Joseph? He'd never do that! Don't worry. Maybe they just suspect him. This doesn't mean he was part of the riots."

There was a knock at the door and Karma went to open it. The Chief of Guard was there but that didn't worry her because a man like her father had many such people come to see him. She welcomed him in and asked him to sit down while she called her father and then she went to her room.

"Hello, Your Honor," said General Graham. "I'm here because of the hearing about the riots tomorrow."

"Don't worry. I've already read the case and it seems that none of the accused are guilty."

"But we want them to be guilty!"

"What do you mean 'we'? Since when do the guards interfere with the judicial system?"

General Graham replied, "The King wants them to be guilty because the King needs to maintain his image, and when the King wants something, he gets it. Do you have a problem with that?"

"But that's illegal!"

"When the King does it, it's legal, Your Honor. We've told them that if they plead guilty, they will get three years in prison and we will pay them well if they serve their time without any trouble. But if they plead not guilty they will face thirty years in prison."

"They know this? You intimidated them? I want to resign now."

"Your Honor, you can't refuse – especially as you have such a lovely daughter."

The Judge understood that they could hurt Karma so he agreed and the General left.

Karma came down and saw her father looking sad – it was the first time she'd seen him that way. She asked if something had happened and what the Chief of Guard wanted from him and he told her it wasn't important.

On the day of the hearing, the accused waited for the Judge to come to announce his decision. The Baker, Hither and Karma were also waiting to hear that Joseph had been found not guilty, and Hither was planning to make a cake for Joseph once he was pardoned to share with him and Karma.

There were twenty-one defendants and twenty pleaded guilty.

"The first defendant?" the Judge said. "How do you plead?"

"Guilty, Your Honor."

"The fifth?"

"Guilty, Your Honor."

"The eleventh?"

"Guilty, Your Honor."

"The seventeenth?"

"Guilty, Your Honor."

"The twenty-first?"

It was now Joseph's turn to plead. General Graham had spoken to him the day before about the deal so Joseph was torn. He could plead guilty and spend three years in prison going against his values and morals by telling a lie and admitting guilt for a crime he didn't commit. That might allow him to go back and marry Karma though he would need to forget about the throne.

He glanced down and saw the bracelet that Mariam gave him when he began his journey and it gave him strength. Joseph pleaded not guilty.

The Judge said, "In the name of the King of Zelaar, I judge all the defendants to be guilty as all were active participants in the riots. "

And the Judge sentenced Joseph to thirty years in prison — everyone was shocked. All his friends — the Baker, Hither, and

Karma – were stunned and were sad because Joseph would go to prison for something he hadn't done.

Joseph had been sorely tempted to plead guilty and forget about the throne and the sword. However, he realized that he didn't know what fate was holding for him in the future, and this might be a call since there is only one moral path to follow. He could accept the call or ignore his father's words about how sometimes he would need to accept the call whether it appeared bad or even good.

The guards escorted Joseph out. As he left, he met Karma's eyes and they seemed to say to him, *Don't worry, you'll be fine.* Then Joseph looked at the Judge who turned away so as to not meet his eyes. The guards pulled Joseph away harshly as people were throwing rocks at the prisoners, and a man yelled, "Rioters deserve to go to prison!"

This situation broke Joseph's heart. He'd told the truth but this is how he was rewarded. As he made his way to prison, for a moment, he lost his interest in life and the throne and for the first time was ready to give up his dream. He was crushed and everything about the sword and seven worriers seemed irrelevant

The guard removed Joseph's handcuffs when they entered the prison and said, "Chief, which cell shall we put him in?"

The Prison Governor answered, "A traitor like him who will spend thirty years with us should go to Cell 42."

They opened Cell 42 and when Joseph entered the cell, the guard said, "This is your cellmate. Please don't bother him because he is very old."

A big tall man with a long white beard welcomed Joseph and said, "Welcome to paradise."

Joseph wondered if his cellmate was sane because no-one would describe prison as a paradise "Paradise?"

"Well, young man, who told you that paradise is in the sky? Paradise is within." He pointed to his chest. "Forgive me. I'm an old man who likes to talk a lot. Let me introduce myself. They call me the Professor."

"Who calls you that?"

"Everyone – it's made me forget my real name." The Professor laughed.

"My name is Joseph."

"It's nice to meet you, young man. Tell me your story about how come you're here in prison. But don't tell me that you didn't do anything and the guard brought you up here unfairly!"

Joseph told him that he wasn't guilty and he looked into the Professor's eyes and fell silent. The guards opened the door and said that their lunch was ready, egg and soup. Joseph didn't want to eat his meal because he was fatigued.

"Young man, if you can't control your mind, it will control you," the Professor said.

Joseph replied angrily, "You don't see where we are! We're in prison! How can you remain so positive?"

"I told you, young man. I see this prison as a sanctuary. If you don't eat, you'll die, and you don't want that."

~   ~   ~

Karma waited for the Judge to arrive home. As soon as he entered the house she said, "Father! What happened today? You knew that Joseph is innocent!"

"It's out of my hands."

THE SEVEN PRINCIPLES

The next day, while the Professor and Joseph were eating breakfast, the Professor tried to break the ice, but Joseph ignored him. Joseph was feeling depressed and had started to lose faith in his destiny. He said to himself, *I'm twenty-three years old and won't leave this prison until I'm fifty-three. It's not worth thinking about being king because I can't do anything about it.*

The Professor decided to not talk and to give him space whenever the guard served the meals, and Joseph remained silent and didn't even make eye contact. After one week, when the Professor saw that Joseph had got used to the prison, he spoke to him. "Young man, if we don't talk, believe me, you'll feel bored and might even consider suicide."

"Well, if I commit suicide, I will know my destiny for sure! Now, my future is uncertain."

"Future! There is no future. Past and future are illusions."

Joseph looked at the ground. "It seems that I have many illusions, so that doesn't shock me."

"Illusions are abstractions of our mind. When I say there is no past or future, I mean that we only have now, the present moment."

"How come there's no future?" asked Joseph.

"Well, when you refer to the future," said the Professor, "you mean the present at that time in the future, but that doesn't mean that the future exists."

"It seems that you're a wise man."

The Professor laughed. "It seems that I will teach you many things, but are you willing to learn?"

"I will learn from you because I have plenty of free time while I'm in prison, and I want to fill that time. It isn't because I'm interested in what you have to say."

"Believe me, you'll enjoy it. Now, you need to tell me your story, the real one."

"I'm not ready to tell you my story unless you want me to make it up!" Joseph said.

The Professor assured Joseph that when he was ready to talk, he would be a good listener and wouldn't judge him and would believe him. At that moment the guards knocked on the door, ready to serve breakfast. Joseph went to take his and the Professor's breakfast, which was one egg and a piece of bread for each of them.

The Professor wanted to see how Joseph reacted when caught unawares. So he threw an egg at Joseph's head.

Joseph was shocked. "What? That's not funny! What are you doing, old man?"

The Professor laughed. "Young man, you need to focus more on your surroundings."

"But usually people in my surroundings don't usually throw eggs!"

"This is your first lesson. The more you're aware of your surroundings, the more you'll be ready for any preemptive attack."

"It's a painful lesson and I'm not sure if I want to learn from you."

"Based on my experience and understanding of life," the Professor replied, "it's no coincidence that you and I are in one place, in one cell."

"But the reason I'm here is that someone has thrown me in prison for something that I haven't done, and I don't believe in coincidences."

"Can you believe that someone also threw *me* in prison for something I didn't do? Isn't that a coincidence?"

"I followed the signs and now I'm here. I haven't gained anything from following my destiny."

"What do you mean, your destiny? How do you know your destiny?" asked the Professor.

"Sometimes I feel a wild desire to chase my fate and sometimes the feeling disappears. If I tell you my real story, you won't believe me."

"And now the second principle," said the Professor. "Let me teach you about the language of desire. You need to listen carefully. What is the language of desire?"

The Professor explained that it was important for people to recognize their destiny and purpose in life, and the way to do this is by listening to our intuition because it knows its path. He told Joseph how it was important to be aware of his desire and ask himself questions such as: *Why does this desire appear now? How is it established? From where did it come? How does it relate to me at this time? Why should I follow it? Why do I have this desire in these circumstances? What if I were born a hundred years earlier or later, would my desire still be the same? How does my desire relate to my environment?*

The Professor paused and said, "Desire is a sign that the soul provides to tell us something we're not aware of. It's an energy of potential that pushes us toward an event, action, or sometimes fate. It sometimes warns us that if we don't interpret our desire correctly, we might make bad decisions or even cause bad events; that we need to identify desire in our mind when we watch our desire."

"These are a lot of questions!" Joseph said. "Why should I ask myself questions?"

"Because everything starts with a good question."

"What if I had a bad desire that pushed me to make a bad decision? Just then, you told me I needed to watch my desire."

"There's bad and good desire. But on balance, we can't categorize desire as good or bad. Desire is desire unless we misinterpret it. Desire guides you to your fate and destiny and complements your thinking. So if you listen to your desire and make a bad decision, that doesn't mean you had a negative desire. It means that you're not aligned with your soul, with your true self. When your desire aligns with positive thinking, you will do good things."

"It seems that I'll learn many things from you, Professor," Joseph replied. "Since you understand the language of desire, what is your desire telling you right now?"

The Professor looked directly into Joseph's eyes and said, "Since your fate and mine are intersecting here in the prison, I need to pass onto you my life experience because you might need it."

Joseph remembered his father's words that he needed to follow the sign. He thought that maybe he should tell his story to the Professor, but he wasn't sure if he wanted to tell him about the sword. Then he decided to be brave and tell him, anyway. No-one else would believe him and he had to spend thirty years in prison. If he didn't tell the Professor now, he would at some point.

"If I tell you my story, you won't accuse me of being crazy or delusional?" asked Joseph.

The Professor smiled and said, "Sometimes it's hard to differentiate between what's real and what's illusion. Feel free to talk and I'll be a good listener."

Joseph related the story about the first time he'd seen the sword when he was eleven and how he'd panicked and thrown it into the forest. Then he told of how a few years later he'd seen it and grabbed it and saw seven warriors circling him, telling him that he was the king and he needed to accept his call because this was his destiny. He described how he'd met Thomas from the circus, met Hither, and worked with the Baker. He talked about going to the castle to serve the King's guests and hearing David conspiring with his Adviser to get rid of the King. Finally, he told of how when the King died, General Graham had accused twenty-one people of being responsible for the riots that happened in the city, telling him that he knew Joseph wasn't involved but he had to plead guilty.

The Professor was shocked and he hugged Joseph and said, "You're Amelia's son!"

"You believe me?"

"I witnessed your birth that night. I witnessed the red moon omen and your mother, the Queen, giving birth. Young man, I told you there is no such thing as coincidence."

"What if I don't become king? What if this isn't my destiny?"

"You're denying your destiny! Usually, people take time to discover their destiny, but in your case, you already know your destiny."

"How come? I'm only a farmer."

"This is your fate, and the more you actualize your destiny, the closer you come to achieving it."

"So I'm not delusional?"

"The question is, would I be delusional if I didn't believe you?" the Professor responded. "Joseph, you're destined to become king."

"If neither of us is delusional, that means I might become king in thirty years from now."

"It depends on you. Only you can postpone your fate."

"Do you mean that I could become king before that?" Joseph asked in surprise.

"Oh, young man, you need to learn a lot of things. Let me teach you the third principle." The Professor explained his third lesson – that Joseph would not fulfill his destiny until he had the experience that qualified him to chase it. He added, "There are two ways to gain experience in life. Either you gain it or someone passes his experience to you. When you gain it, there are two paths – you gain it because you understand it or through suffering."

"I don't understand why I need experience to fulfill my destiny? In the end, my destiny is my destiny! Logically speaking, it's something that will happen whether I accept it or not, isn't it?"

"Your destiny is a path that includes events, people, cycles, and your goals."

"I don't understand, Professor," said Joseph. "You make it hard for me."

"Each of us here on Earth has their own fate and destiny," said the Professor. "Therefore, each of us has our own challenges and difficulties that indicate our purpose. Your destiny is to become king, and to be king, you need to have an experience that will qualify you to fill that position."

"Did you face difficulty when you pursued your destiny?"

"Do you remember the first principle I taught you?" asked the Professor.

"Yes, about the language of desire! But why do you mention that while teaching me the third principle?"

"From that principle, I learned that I had a desire to pursue the path of knowledge, but my difficulty was that I couldn't learn fast – that was my challenge. Therefore, I spent more time on it and tried to find ways to overcome this challenge. The more I failed, the more I learned, and the more I experienced"

"I thought that the principles you taught weren't related to each other?"

"Knowledge is a huge part of our accumulated experience. The more knowledge you have, the greater the chance that you will fulfill your destiny."

"Do I need to have tons of accumulated experience in life to chase my destiny?" Joseph asked.

"It's always good to have plenty of experience, but you need to chase your own experience. My experience might give you better judgment, but it might not help you toward achieving your destiny."

"How do I find my own experience?"

"You need to observe the signs that appear in your journey to regain your rightful inheritance," said the Professor.

"So, if you pass me your experience onto me that means that I will become king sooner?"

"I didn't say you will become king sooner," the Professor replied, "but if you gain the experience that will qualify you to be king sooner, you might. I don't think there's anything that will prevent you from becoming king sooner if you've already gained the experience to qualify you to become king."

"Share your experience with me now, then," Joseph said.

"If you had the experience you needed, you wouldn't ask me this. You need to reconcile with fate."

"How can I reconcile with fate?"

"You have to be ready!"

"How?"

"When you have the accumulated experience that qualifies you to move a step toward your destiny," the Professor said.

"Why do I need to be qualified?"

"Because when you're qualified, fate will respond to you!"

"What if it doesn't?"

"That's means you aren't ready yet!" said the Professor. "To be ready means you're done with that particular experience, which also means you've absorbed it. That experience might be a challenge and sometimes a difficulty. If you overcome it, you'll move another step toward your destiny."

"What if I'm ready but fate doesn't respond?"

"If you've convinced yourself that you're ready and you're not, you're only manipulating yourself – you can't manipulate fate.

"Professor! You're making this so hard for me," Joseph said petulantly.

"You need to be patient because everything comes from patience."

~ ~ ~

King David was sitting on his throne enjoying being king. Beside him was the Bad Adviser, who saw his dream become manifest. The Bad Adviser didn't care if David was a good or bad king, because the most important fact for him was that he could achieve his dream of becoming the King's Adviser. He wished that *he* could be the king, but that was impossible – he had to accept that with him not being of royal blood, it could never happen. But the position of the King's Adviser was the most influential position in the kingdom and he could push for anything he wanted to achieve, whether in his own or the King's best interests.

David said, "How is my kingdom faring?"

"Your Majesty," said the Bad Adviser, "everything is going perfectly and the citizens wish you all the best in your reign."

"As I don't have that much experience, I'll need you beside me all the time. Do you understand?"

The Bad Adviser bowed and said, "Your wish is my command, Your Majesty," and then he left.

Isabella entered and greeted David. "I was wondering if the Professor was coming from his trip soon," she said, "because he's missed many events such as Father's death and your coronation."

David couldn't tell her the truth because the truth would be too hard for her. And it would mean that the whole kingdom would find out that David had poisoned his father to become king. He decided that the best course of action was to assign the Chief of Guard to search for and bring back the Professor.

~ ~ ~

The Bad Adviser had returned to his office and was thinking about his new position and the power that he had and the power he would gain. The idea of David abandoning him in the future occurred to him, and after pondering on the idea he thought it was possible that one day David would abandon him once David felt confident in the power he held, and their plan was the only insurance between them. He needed a plan to ensure that David didn't feel that he could replace him at any time and for any reason. After thinking for a long time, he couldn't find a plan better than the old one which was to create chaos and be the one who resolved the situation. This would require collaboration with the gang leader again, and the Bad Adviser needed to offer something in return, so he needed to become more powerful.

~   ~   ~

That night Joseph was lying in bed following his daily routine of thinking about everything that had happened that day. He was thinking about his foster family, the throne, and Karma, and he said in a loud voice, "It isn't fair."

The Professor heard him and felt that Joseph's tone revealed many things so he got out of bed and went to talk with him. "Young man, why can't you fall asleep tonight?"

"Professor, I don't know why this has happened to me. Is it my fate to be king?"

"It seems I must give you your fourth principle in the middle of the night. You will understand your fate by understanding your circumstances."

"Circumstances! Don't you see where we are right now?"

"Your circumstances are a preparation, not an ordeal. If you see them as an ordeal, you'll learn nothing but will simply feel stressed."

Joseph: "How I can do it?"

"By asking questions!"

"What questions?"

"Look where we are right now," said the Professor, "and see how this is related to your destiny of gaining the throne. How do these circumstances help you move forward? What do you need to learn in this step?"

"Okay! I'm in prison with you, and because of that I'm aware more of my destiny."

"And?"

"And I'm sure I'm not delusional about seeing the seven warriors."

"Believe me, there are many reasons. Maybe one of the reasons is that I can share with you my experience, but still this is an outer reason."

"Outer reason? That means there is an inner reason, doesn't it?" Joseph asked.

"This is what I intended to do, to shift your focus to the inner reason. Think of the questions that I shared with you and try to go deeper into yourself and reflect on those questions in your inner world. There you will find your answers."

"But Professor, I'm not looking for answers! I'm looking for questions, so why do we need to ask questions?"

"Because the most important thing in life is to ask the right question. If you ask the right question, you'll get the right answer. You get what you ask for."

"If I ask the right question how I will receive the right answer?" Joseph asked.

"By observation!"

"Why do I need to observe?"

"Let me ask you a question," said the Professor. "How do you think people discover how everything works or what the characteristics of human nature are?"

"By observing?"

"Yes! Those who discovered these facts are people who observed and pondered about what was happening at that moment."

"There is a question that I don't have an answer to," said Joseph. "There's a girl I met called Karma and I don't know if I love her or I like her. It is hard to differentiate. I feel lost because of this question. And it's her right to know if I love her or like her."

"So you asked a proper question, but you didn't receive a proper answer? That means you asked the first part correctly, but you failed in the second part. Which means that you didn't remove yourself from reality."

"Why should I remove myself from reality?"

"To see it as it is."

Joseph sighed and said, "If I love Karma, why do I feel this is a hard question to answer?"

"Joseph, believe me you know the answer, but you need to dig deep within. The answer is there, you need only to recognize it."

"How come the answer I seek is inside me?"

"And now the fifth principle. The answers you seek are inside you. The louder the whisper becomes the closer you get to it. Therefore, you and your answer seek each other at the same time."

"How does the answer seek me?"

"It will search for you when the whispers become louder," the Professor answered:

"The Oracle said I will meet my twin flame and I think Karma is the perfect woman and will suit me as my future queen."

"Do you love her or are you trying to convince yourself that you love her because of the Oracle's words? But I'm an old man who needs his sleep. When you stop chasing love, love will find you."

The next day Joseph woke up and saw the Professor waiting for the guard to bring their breakfast, so he greeted him. The guard knocked on the door and passed them one egg each and one piece of bread. The Professor told Joseph that he'd asked the guard to not cook Joseph's egg.

"I don't understand. Do you want me to eat raw egg?" asked Joseph.

"You accept that I'm teaching you about life? The first thing you need to master is how to remove the eggshell using a fork without damaging the inside because if you do that you'll end up wetting your clothes with raw egg."

"But what could I learn from this?" Joseph replied. "I'm supposed to eat the egg not just remove the outer layer. Plus if I don't eat it I'll be hungry before lunchtime."

The Professor told Joseph that if he could remove the shell without breaking the egg, he would sacrifice his breakfast for one month. Joseph accepted the challenge. On his first attempt, Joseph's hand started to shake and the egg broke making his clothes wet and he failed the challenge. The Professor told Joseph he needed to try again the next day and reminded him that he would not teach him more until he'd completed this task.

For thirty-three days Joseph tried to remove the eggshell while the Professor silently watched him. Something happened that day to make Joseph lose control because he felt he was wasting his time, that he would spend thirty years of his life in prison. He said to himself, *What are the odds that I'll get out?* Joseph threw the egg and started to scream at the Professor. The noise made the guards come running to see what the problem was.

Two guards entered Cell 42 and the first said, "What's your problem, prisoner? You don't like this place? Or do you miss your mammy?" He laughed.

The second guard said, "Prisoner, you'll be spending thirty years with us and you need to learn self-control or we'll have to find a way to teach it to you!"

The Prison Governor entered and the guards explained to him what had happened. The chief said, "Send him into solitary confinement for one week"

Joseph said, "I didn't do anything," but these were the rules of the prison. The guards handcuffed Joseph as the Professor looked into Joseph's eyes. It was as if his eyes said, *Don't worry. It will pass.*

The guards took Joseph to another building. As they entered, Joseph couldn't hear anything. It was very quiet in a way that could make people go insane. They opened a cell door and threw Joseph in saying, "You're here for one week. Next time it will be one month, and if we need to bring you here again it will be one year. Do you understand, prisoner?"

No light could enter the cell and the silence quiet scared Joseph, as did having no cellmate to talk to. After a while, a guard knocked on the door and slid in Joseph's breakfast. Joseph saw the food, but he had no appetite, so he didn't eat it. At dinner time a guard knocked on the door and opened a small slot, waiting for Joseph to return his breakfast plate in exchange for dinner. Joseph passed his breakfast plate through the opening.

"Hey, you," said the guard. "Why didn't you eat your breakfast?"

"I don't know. I didn't feel like eating."

"They told me it's your first time in solitary confinement. I know it's hard but you need to eat."

Joseph felt that he knew this guy and said, "Your voice is familiar. Do I know you?" Then he realized. "I know you – you're Richard!"

"How could you know me from just my voice? Do you really know me?"

"I'm Joseph from the bakery. It's a long story. So you got your job back?"

"Because of you," said Richard.

"Please tell me that you'll be here all the time," said Joseph, "because I hate this place and am so bored."

"I'm on the night shift. How come you're here?"

"Would you believe that I'm here for something that I didn't do? General Graham accused me of being involved in the riots!"

"That's horrible. Is prison hard for you?"

"Only when the Professor isn't here."

"That tall man with a white beard?" asked Richard. "That was the man who gave me food for months! Believe me, he's an honorable man."

Joseph told Richard he needed to sleep, and he lay in bed thinking about his day from morning till night. He thought about what a coincidence it was that he'd met the Professor who'd been the King's Adviser, his father's Adviser, and suddenly was his cellmate. Plus, how the person who he'd given one third of his money to was now the person who was responsible – everything is related to everything else.

On the second day the guard knocked the door and passed through his breakfast so Joseph ate it. But when it was time for lunch no-one appeared so he waited for dinner. Richard knocked on the door to announce he was there.

"Richard, why didn't anyone give me lunch?" asked Joseph,

"Welcome to solitary confinement! We only provide two meals here – breakfast and dinner."

Joseph was happy that he and Richard could talk and he wouldn't feel lonely in solitary confinement. Joseph said to Richard, "I want to share something with you but I don't know if you'll believe me!"

"Why shouldn't I believe you? Please talk. I'm a good listener and I owe you."

Joseph told him his story from the day when he'd been eleven years old, the circus, the Baker, the King's ceremony, and the day the Chief of Guards had accused him and taken him to the prison.

"Wait a second," said Richard in amazement. "Are you telling me that you're the true king and your father was the King and your mother the Queen who died twenty-three years ago?"

"Believe it or not, this is the truth, and I don't know why the Professor is leading me to believe that I could leave this prison before my thirty years is up."

"The Professor is a wise man and knows many things."

"He tells me that everything is connected and there is no coincidence but I don't understand what he means. Now I need to go to bed to sleep because if I don't get into bed, I'll fall asleep on the floor and it's painful to sleep on the floor!"

On the third day as the guard passed Joseph his breakfast, Joseph asked his guard for a raw egg instead of a cooked one. The guard was shocked and laughed at the idea of someone wanting a raw egg instead of a cooked one but handed it to him regardless.

Joseph took the egg and tried to remove the shell without breaking the egg and he failed – and his clothes soon smelled of egg

– but he decided to not give up and to master the task the Professor had given him. That night Richard came by to give him his dinner and they talked.

On the sixth day in solitary confinement, when the guard gave Joseph his breakfast Joseph decided to not think about anything except one thing – the egg. After forty attempts since he first started the challenge in Cell 42, Joseph succeeded in removing the shell and leaving the egg unbroken. He felt a sense of accomplishment because of what he'd done and could hardly wait until the next day when he could show the Professor how he'd done it.

That night Richard brought Joseph his dinner for the last time. Richard said, "Joseph, I have an idea that could get you out of prison but you might not like it. I felt that I should do something for you because you helped me, but I will need to put myself in prison if they discover it and you need to trust me."

"What's your plan?"

"You need to do something violent when you return so they'll send you to solitary confinement for one month. Then I will try to help you to escape. And every night I'll put an empty plate through the slot so the guards will give you the breakfast in the morning and at night I'll throw it away."

"They'll accuse you of helping me to escape because you're responsible for the prisoners in solitary confinement!" Joseph said.

"They've accused me of doing something I didn't do," Richard said, "and this time they'll accuse me of something I actually did."

"Why do you want to help me?"

"You and the Professor both helped me and I owe you and I need to pay my debt. Don't you remember when we were in the bakery? I told you that one day I would repay my debt."

The next morning the guard came for Joseph and escorted him back to Cell 42 where he saw the Professor. He had in his hand the egg without its shell.

The Professor greeted Joseph. "Young man, you're back."

Joseph raised his hand proudly to show the Professor the egg. "I did it!"

"I knew it you could do it," the Professor said. He asked Joseph about how solitary confinement had been and Joseph told him about everything and about how he'd met Richard, the person he'd given a third of his money to in the middle of the night. The Professor reminded Joseph that there are no coincidences and everything means something; all things are related to all other things because everything is connected like the threads in a fabric. Joseph felt that there was a higher power that guides us as humans, but he didn't know how it worked. Then he told the Professor about Richard's plan to help him escape.

The Professor said, "Are you ready to go to the unknown?"

"What do you mean? I'm leaving and this is what I want."

"You don't know what your life will be after you leave because your next journey would be full of unpredictable events, so are you willing to follow the sign toward your life's purpose?"

"What if they catch me and kill me because I escaped from prison?" Joseph asked.

"What you will face is that for a moment that you will feel as if you are going to die, but this is only an illusion, Joseph."

"So what happens when someone kills us?"

"Spiritually speaking, there is no term for death; death is an illusion that humanity has created for themselves." After a pause, the Professor added, "Imagine being dead. You've gone from this world and lost everything – money, family, and even yourself. If you return to reality, what's the first thing you'll do?"

Joseph thought for a moment and said, "Get back my throne." He understood that the Professor was telling him that if we remove fear from our minds, we can better focus on chasing our purpose in life. Joseph was grateful for everything the Professor had taught him, but he was curious about the Professor's life, as well as his birth family, and why his mother had sacrificed him. In response to his questions, the Professor told Joseph that he'd served his father the King and his grandfather the King before him through fifty years of service. He'd been in charge of managing any transitional phase between one king and another because there were traditions that had to be observed. The Professor then told him about his sister Isabella and his half-brother David. The Professor was answerable to Isabella, and the Kings' assistant, who was now David's adviser and in charge of David's affairs.

Joseph wondered aloud why David's adviser had got rid of the King to put David on the throne so he could become the King's Adviser.

"Greed makes people dissatisfied about what they own because they want more, and when they get more they want still more," the Professor said.

"But how did David's Adviser know that David wouldn't be king until he held the sword? I don't understand."

"When someone lets greed into their life, they won't be satisfied with anything. Thirty years ago, I saw David's adviser in a shelter, and he gained my attention because he was clever so I adopted him so he could work with me."

"But he knew about the prophecy about the future king and the sword. Is that right?

"You're ready for me to teach you the seventh principle," the Professor said, "which is that when people start to chase a purpose that isn't their purpose in life, they believe that the ends justify the means."

"What's the relationship between greed and our purpose in life?"

"Each of us on Earth has our own fate and destiny. You have a purpose that fits your abilities. Therefore, each person is created for a reason that fits their time and place."

"So the easiest way to know our purpose is to look at our abilities?"

"Yes. You'll be successful if you align with your purpose, but when you chase a purpose that isn't your true purpose, you won't succeed because that purpose doesn't fit your abilities."

"So what's easy for me is my purpose?" asked Joseph.

"When you're chasing your purpose in life, say, a job or position, it will be easy for you because even if you feel blue one day, you'll perform well. But when people start to chase a purpose that isn't their purpose in life, it's hard and stressful for them. For example, if I became the Chief of Guard one day, I'd fail because it doesn't fit my abilities unless this position lures me. So I might believe the ends justify the means."

"Like David's adviser?"

"Yes," said the Professor. "When people start to chase a purpose that isn't their life purpose, they will apply 'the ends justify the means' like David's adviser did. He felt stressed planning and breaking the rules to achieve a purpose that wasn't meant for him. He used unethical approaches to chase that goal, to seek power."

Then the Professor told him the reason why his mother had sacrificed him when she gave birth, because of the prophecy. He mentioned that there was a book called *The Testament of Flame*, and in it was mentioned there is a prophecy said that once a century, when the Queen was giving birth and the moon was red, she needed to sacrifice her male child by giving him away. This sacrifice was meant to protect and prepare the future king by having him live with his people, as part of them. It would enable him to sees the weaknesses of society, to ensure he was from the people and would act for the people and would purify the kingdom from injustice and spread peace.

Over the next three months, Joseph learned how to read and write, and learned about many subjects such as philosophy, politics, and science, from the Professor. This changed Joseph's perspective and his way of thinking; he'd learned that everything starts from within and that life is only an abstraction of our self – it doesn't fall in line with our perceptions, but rather our perceptions align with life.

The Professor asked, "Joseph, do you think I've taught you anything?"

"I am in your debt you because you've taught me many things."

The Professor thought for a moment and said, "What would you say if I told you I haven't taught you anything because you already knew these things? It was only a matter of shifting your focus to something deeper."

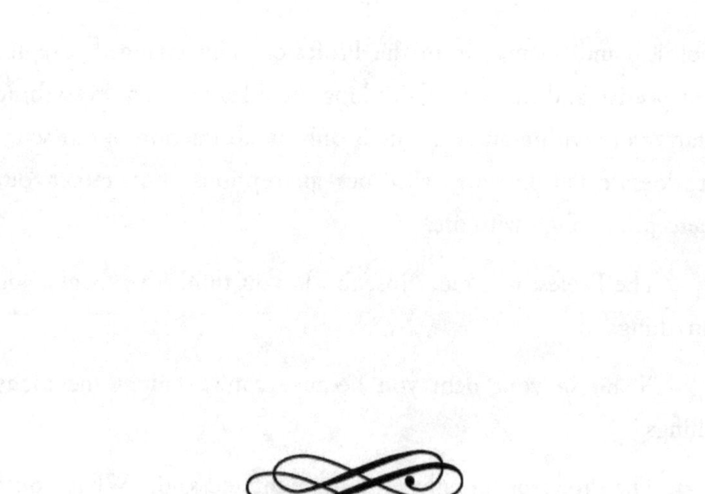

Ticket to the Unknown

J oseph was ready to go to solitary confinement where Richard was waiting for his signal.

"It's time, Professor," Joseph said

"Time for what?"

"I need to do something and you'll need to forgive me. But I need to do it!"

"Do what?" the Professor asked, exasperated.

"I need to punch your face so the guard will send me back into solitary confinement."

"Is that really necessary?"

"I think so."

"Well, please be gentle."

Joseph punched the Professor and shouted in a threatening manner to gain the guards' attention and the Professor shouted,

"Help me! I've been punched in my face! I'm an old man and he's punching me!"

The guards soon arrived and Joseph was given one month's solitary confinement as punishment.

He waited until Richard came to give him his dinner.

"Whenever you're ready tell me, and I will help you escape, even tonight," Richard said.

"I don't think I want to escape tonight because I want a few days in solitary."

"The more we wait, the more we lose the advantage."

"I want to use the time in the solitary to think about an important matter," said Joseph.

"As you wish. I'll give you your space."

For twenty-one nights Joseph remained silent and considered his thoughts and any ideas that occurred to him. He asked himself questions such as whether or not he loved Karma, if he'd learned enough to pursue his purpose, what he should do next, and what sort of person he needed to be for his next journey.

Then after spending three months and eleven days in prison, he gave Richards the signal that he wanted to escape. Richard quietly opened the cell door and they went to the courtyard away from the guards. Richard escorted Joseph to a spot where no-one would notice him. He opened the door and they went outside. This was the moment that Joseph should run but he didn't know in which direction to go.

"Go north," said Richard, "and you'll be in another city soon. I hope you'll be safe. I've now repaid my debt. To be honest, I don't know why I did this, Joseph, except I felt it was the best thing to do."

"Thank you for taking this risk for me," said Joseph. "I hope that one day we'll meet in better circumstances."

They hugged each other and Joseph walked away. He couldn't go north to the other city but needed to go south first so he could see Karma, the Baker, and Hither to tell them that he was out of prison before he could pursue his journey. The city was forty-two miles away and it would take at least eight hours to walk there. Darkness had begun to fall and he knew it was very dangerous to go to the city and risk someone seeing him, but he had decided to take that risk.

In the dead of night, Joseph arrived in the city and went straight to the Judge's house. Once he'd arrived, he threw stones at Karma's bedroom window to wake her. Karma heard the noise and opened the window, looking out.

Joseph called, "Karma, Karma, Karma."

Karma went outside and said, "Joseph! What are you doing here? I don't understand. Aren't you supposed to be in prison?"

"It's a long story. I walked to see you and tell you that you're a lovely woman, and you deserve a true love story. But I don't know if I like you or love you, even though I've tried so hard to search within myself for the answer."

"Is it so hard to decide?"

"Believe me it is difficult, especially when yours and my destiny are intertwined. I don't want to look like I'm selfish, but you're precious to me and I'm not ready to lose either you or my destiny. I fear that I might lose you if I choose my destiny or lose my destiny if I choose you."

Karma moved closer to him and touched Joseph's hand while gazing into his eyes. "Joseph, please don't worry," she said. "I completely understand what you're saying but now you should focus on what you're going to do next."

"I don't know if you are my twin flame or not, but what I know for sure is that if you are my twin flame – time, place, and circumstance are irrelevant."

"You're a good man, Joseph," Karma said, "and any girl would want to be with you. I would be a lucky woman if you were my twin flame."

"I'm fearful to take this step even though I do believe that you are my twin flame!"

"Will this help you to actualize your destiny?"

"I fear it does! What I should do to focus on my journey is free you and let fate decide if we will reunite, because what is meant to be is inevitable," said Joseph.

"So let both of us surrender our union to fate?"

"What if –"

"What if we triumph!" interrupted Karma.

Joseph said goodbye to Karma and went straight to the Baker and Hither. He stealthily entered the bakery from the stable. Hither heard someone was there so she went down and saw Joseph. She immediately went to the Baker and woke him.

"Joseph!" said the Baker once he was with Joseph. "I don't understand. Aren't you supposed to be in prison?"

"Yes, but I escaped and I need to share something with you and Hither."

Joseph told them the story about the sword and the seven warriors, and how the King was his father. They found it hard to believe the story as it sounded like a fantasy, but because they knew Joseph was an honest person, they decided to believe him. The Baker asked Joseph if he needed any help and Joseph told him that he was there to collect the rest of his money, the last third of the money his foster father had given him. He asked the Baker if he could leave his sword with him because he'd need it in the future. The Baker asked Joseph to walk with him to the stable and offered him the horse he'd seen before.

"I told you that one day this horse would be yours," the Baker said to Joseph.

"But, sir, this is too much."

"You need to take it or I'll be mad at you. You have a long journey and within a few hours it will be sunrise and you need to leave the city soon."

Joseph thanked the Baker and said goodbye. He mounted the horse and went north. Although he didn't know what would happen next, he did know that it would be far better than what was happening at the present moment. He believed in his journey and walking into the unknown, knowing and trusting the process and fate to fulfill his purpose and destiny.

When Joseph was far from the city and the sun had begun to rise, he decided to walk slowly and enjoy the nature surrounding him. Suddenly, a group of five people came from nowhere, surrounding him and pointing their swords and knives at him. Joseph stood still.

One of the highwaymen said in an evil voice, "Stop there, young man."

"What do you want from me and why have you pointed your swords and knives at me?" asked Joseph.

One of the highwaymen said, "This is not your lucky day. Dismount from your horse and give us all your money."

Joseph stuttered, "But if I give you my money, I won't have anything left. And the horse isn't mine."

Another of the highwaymen said, "So you're a thief?" He turned to his companions and added, "Let's kill him and take his money."

"Please take my money and don't kill me, please," Joseph said.

Joseph was fearful because he didn't want to die, and he couldn't do anything because they were a group and he was alone. One of the highwaymen seemed to sympathize with Joseph and said they should let him go since they'd got his money and the horse, which looked like a thoroughbred. He said, "Let the boy go. I don't think we'll benefit from killing him."

They let Joseph go and he ran north, frightened but happy to still be alive. After a while, he slowed down. He suddenly found himself on the road the caravans used and every caravan he saw he asked if he could go with them.

He called out to the first caravan, "Sir, may I go with you?"

The person in the caravan said, "Give me five coins or I won't let you."

After one hour he saw another caravan and asked, "Sir, may I go with you?"

The person in the caravan said, "You look creepy, young man, and I don't let strangers into my caravan."

Joseph was feeling anxious and tired when he heard someone call his name. "Joseph! I think it's you? Joseph!"

He looked around to see the Wheat Supplier in his caravan, The Wheat Supplier asked why Joseph was walking in this place. Joseph started to tell him the story of escaping the prison and how the Chief of Guards had accused him unfairly. The wheat supplier believed him because he knew that the Baker, who he'd known for many decades, didn't let anyone work with him unless he was sure that person was decent and honest. "Are you hungry? Do you want a sandwich?" he asked.

"I'm starving. Thanks," said Joseph.

"So where are you heading?"

"I don't know, but for sure another city where I can restart my life."

After a few hours, they'd arrived in the Kingdom of Ostax where they embarked in the main market where there were many old buildings, a bazaar, and people who sold fabric and vegetables. The Wheat Supplier wanted to drop off items that he'd bought in Joseph's kingdom. He said, "Joseph, this is my hometown, and I hope you'll like it. Don't worry about anything. You will be my guest for a few days."

"Thank you, sir. I am so grateful that you're going to help me."

"You're under my watch, and no-one will do anything to you. Let's go to my cottage, and please call me Mr. Hall."

They went to the cottage and Mr. Hall's wife greeted Joseph and asked him if he wanted anything to eat. Joseph was starving because apart from the sandwich the Wheat Supplier had given him, the last time he'd eaten was at breakfast in the prison. Mrs. Hall was welcoming and made him a small snack and chatted to him, asking about his trip and what he planned to do next. Then Mr. Hall showed Joseph a small room in his cottage and told him that he could sleep there that night. Joseph looked around the room and thought about his bed at his foster family's house, his bed in the Baker's stable, and his bed in the prison with the Professor. He started to look forward to the time when he wasn't roaming around the country and would have one place in which to permanently sleep and live.

The next morning Mrs. Hall made a delicious breakfast for them and Mr. Hall asked Joseph to go with him to the main market in the city. They headed to the Antique Merchant because the Wheat Supplier wanted to introduce Joseph to him as the Merchant might be able to offer him a job. Mr. Hall and the Merchant had been friends for decades, and he was the only man he would trust with Joseph.

They entered the Antique Merchant's shop and Mr. Hall said, "Hello there. It's been a while since I've seen you."

The Antique Merchant was checking some merchandise when he heard his friend's voice and said, "How are you? And who is this gentleman?"

"This gentleman is called Joseph and he's a decent man. I'm hoping you can find a job for him. Believe me, he's an intelligent person."

The Merchant turned to Joseph and said, "Mr. Hall has never let me down so I'll offer you a job here in my shop."

Joseph was filled with happiness. "I'm ready now," he said. "I'll do whatever you want, sir. Thank you for offering me a job."

The Antique Merchant said, "You remind of me when I was young, when the Wheat Supplier and I were very energetic and felt we could do anything. I like this about you, Joseph."

"We've had our fun and it's the young people's turn to enjoy life," said Mr. Hall.

Mr. Hall had to leave to deal with a business matter so the Antique Merchant and Joseph decided to get to know each other.

While they were chatting, someone entered the store, saying, "Hi, Father."

"You've been missing for two days, Robert,' said the Antique Merchant.

"I was with my friends." He pointed at Joseph. "Who is this person?"

The Antique Merchant said, "This is Joseph and he will work with us in the shop."

"But, Father, I've been telling you for a long time that I wanted to work with you in the shop," Robert said angrily, "and you never let me. And now you've brought in someone you don't know to work with you? It isn't fair! I don't know if you are really my father."

When Robert went out again, the Antique Merchant moved closer to Joseph and said, "You shouldn't worry about Robert. He's just stubborn. You can start work tomorrow."

"Again, thank you, sir, for offering me the job," Joseph said.

He made his way back to the cottage and when he arrived Mrs. Hall was preparing lunch. "So, did you get a job?" she asked.

"Yes, the Antique Merchant is a generous man."

"And does his generosity include a place to live?"

"No, it was only a job."

The Wheat Supplier returned and they sat at the table to eat lunch. Mrs. Hall said to her husband, "Did you knew that Joseph has got a job?"

"Yes, I knew. He is a clever young man."

Joseph smiled.

"And did you know that the Antique Merchant hasn't offered him a place to stay? I was wondering if he would share the cost of living with us – before we were two and now we are three."

Mr. Hall looked angry and said, "Not now!"

Joseph felt that the atmosphere had changed so he finished his meal quickly and went to his room. He could hear the Wheat Supplier and his wife arguing.

"Why did you say that in front of him?" Mr. Hall asked.

"Since your farm has been vandalized because of the weather, we've had financial problems. If he wants to stay with us, he needs to pay."

Mr. Hall sounded upset when he said, "You're always like this and you won't change."

Mr. Hall went to Joseph's room and sat on the bed. "Joseph, I'm sorry if you heard that. I am so sorry."

"Mr. Hall, believe me, it's okay and Mrs. Hall is right. I need to contribute toward costs once I get paid by the Antique Merchant."

"You don't have to! The Baker has supported me many times and now I need to return the favor by taking care of you."

The Wheat Supplier gave Joseph space so he could rest. While he was lying in bed he performed his daily routine of was thinking about everything without knowing what would come next. He recalled the questions the Professor had taught him and asked himself, *What's next? How do these circumstances relate to my goal? What should I do right now?*

The next day Joseph woke up and prepared himself for his first day of working in the Antique Merchant's shop. When he arrived, the Antique Merchant was dealing with a customer. He noticed Joseph and told him to wait. When he'd finished, he said, "Hello, young man. Are you ready for your first day?"

"Yes, sir. Just tell me what I should do."

"It seems that you are a sociable person and you can communicate well with customers so I want you to be a salesman."

The Antique Merchant sold everything to do with antiques and his customers came from around the city and other kingdoms. On his first day, Joseph was happy with his job. The Antique Merchant watched Joseph from a distance, watched how he interacted with customers and how he easily broke the ice with them. Joseph made his first sale which impressed the Antique Merchant. The customer had bought an expensive antique because of Joseph's salesmanship skills. Joseph had shown that he was qualified for the job because he could understand the customer's wants and needs.

The Antique Merchant told Joseph that he would give him a small commission for what he'd sold, telling him that he deserved it. At that moment Robert entered the shop and saw his father giving Joseph some money.

Robert said in a loud voice, "Father, what is this? Why are you giving Joseph money? Don't you usually give your employees their wages at the end of the month?"

"It's his commission, Robert! You knew that the seller gets a small commission and he deserves it because he sold a very old antique." And then the Antique Merchant went to grab something from his friend the butcher.

"I know what you're doing, Joseph," Robert said once they were alone.

"I don't understand what you mean."

"I won't let you steal his business from my father – my future business."

"I don't want to steal anything, Robert. I'm an employee."

Joseph felt that there was something wrong with Robert but he wasn't sure what it was, so he decided to not think about it and focus on cleaning some antiques. At the end of the day, the Antique Merchant came to Joseph to congratulate him on finishing his first day in the shop.

After a month of Joseph working for him, the Antique Merchant was still impressed and Robert became more jealous of Joseph as each day passed. Joseph avoided any contact with Robert because he felt that Robert didn't like him.

~ ~ ~

In the castle, the Bad Adviser had started to execute his first plan to empower himself. He knew that David was inadequate as king and feared that one day that David would surrender him as an adviser. The Bad Adviser went to the gang leader and told him that he wanted a few activists to go to the city and show their dislike of David's policies.

"It seems that you ask more than you give, Adviser, and this it should be a partnership," the gang leader said to him.

"Don't be greedy!"

"Look who's talking about being greedy! You're the one who's doing their all to be the King's Adviser," the gang leader replied mockingly.

"At the right time, I will reward you with something that you make you happy, but now I need you to follow my orders," the Bad Adviser said.

"As you wish, Adviser!"

Within a few days, a group of people had gone to the city and were loudly yelling their disapproval of the King's policies. King David called for his Adviser. When he arrived, he said to him, "What is the hell is going on?"

"Your Majesty, people will talk whether you are good or bad. I suggest that you don't waste your attention and time on them."

"Should I be worried about this?"

"Your Majesty, they are but a few activists showing their disapproval of the King's policies."

"It isn't a good idea to arrest them because that could damage your reputation as you're new to the throne."

The Bad Adviser's plan was to wait for David to tell him that he needed his help so he could show him that his help was essential. He knew that if David didn't ask him to solve the problem this time, he would next time because David was impatient and he was much attached to the idea of being king. After this meeting, the Bad Adviser sent a message to the gang leader to increase the number of activists in the city.

Within two days, David had heard that the number of activists had increased, so he asked his Adviser to discuss the matter with him. " You told me I don't need to pay them any attention but now they're a threat. I don't know why I assigned you as my adviser. Aren't you supposed to solve my problems?" David said.

"You didn't ask me to solve it, Your Majesty. If you want it resolved just ask me and consider it done," said the Bad Adviser as he bowed.

The Bad Adviser sent the gang leader a massage that said: "End it now". Immediately, the gang leader told his people to return home. All the activists were members of the gang or from other gangs that the gang leader had paid them from his own pocket, assuming there'd be future favors from the Bad Adviser once he had empowered himself more.

Once King David discovered there were no longer activists in the city, and his image had been maintained, he started to trust his adviser more than before. The Bad Adviser was happy with this but he wasn't satisfied yet – he wanted more, more than before.

The Bad Adviser orchestrated more fake riots, conflict, and news so David felt captive to his adviser's counsel.

JEALOUSY INCARNATE

For months Joseph showed so much loyalty toward and did so much outstanding work and created so much profit for the Antique Merchant that he started to trust Joseph even more than ever, which made Robert more jealous.

Robert became so anxious that his friends noticed. He said to one of his friends, "One day, I will kill this Joseph. He's driving me nuts."

"I don't know why you worry about him so much. He doesn't deserve your attention."

"Since I was young my dream's been to manage the shop once my father becomes old and now Joseph will take control of it!"

His friend worried about him and discussed it behind Robert's back, saying that his behavior was unacceptable, especially his saying that he would do something bad in the future to Joseph. But they didn't give the matter too much importance because they knew Robert's ego was big but he was a good person inside and no real threat to anyone.

One day, the Antique Merchant saw Joseph taking a break, so he decided to have a chat with him, asking him about his work and telling him that his sales could increase because of him. He said, "Hey, Joseph. How was your day?"

"Sir, it was perfect and one of the merchants sent you a package."

"Did it come today? Yes, it's Tuesday! I'd completely forgotten about it. Thank you for taking it in."

"Sir, it's my job. I put it in the shop."

"Good job, young man," the Antique Merchant said. "I was thinking that if you want, I could make you cashier?"

"Sir, that would be a huge responsibility. I don't know if I'm ready for it."

"Believe me, you were born for this job. You've already done good work. And don't worry, I'll pay you more."

Joseph was happy that the Antique Merchant had started to trust him more and that he would make more money than before.

The next day Robert entered the shop and saw Joseph was working as the cashier. He yelled, "Why are you the cashier? Aren't you supposed to be a salesman working with my father?"

Joseph told him that his father had assigned him the role of cashier as well as salesman. Later that day, Joseph was closing the shop as usual and Robert went to his father to talk to him. He said, "Father, why are you treating Joseph like this? I feel like I'm not your only son and you trust him more than me."

"Joseph showed competence," the Antique Merchant said, "but you don't know how to do anything in life, only taking money from me and hanging out with your friends. You've never taken your life seriously."

Robert felt threatened by Joseph so he decided to lie to his father. "Did you know that Joseph was selling antiques at a lower price in exchange for anther commission from him? He took two commissions at one time."

"When you will stop being delusional?" the Merchant said. He didn't believe Robert and decided to ignore him.

~ ~ ~

In the castle the Bad Adviser was feeling his power increase over King David. Day by day, David was more bound to his adviser's counsel. The Bad Adviser went to David to remind him that guests from another kingdom were due to arrive the next week and he needed to welcome them, emphasizing how important it was to improve the relationship between the two kingdoms. He said, "It's important that you're ready to give a speech."

"I don't have time to write a speech," David replied. "You write it because I don't know how to do it."

"Your wish is my command, Your Majesty."

David was lost because he knew that he wasn't capable of being a good king, but he couldn't come to terms with this fact because of his ego. Although the Bad Adviser was feeling empowered and seeking more power than before, he was still not satisfied – he would never be satisfied.

After one week, the Bad Adviser wrote a speech for David to enable him to maintain his image in front of his guests. The Bad Adviser needed to show the public that David was a good king, but in reality, behind closed doors, David was in thrall to his Adviser. Before the reception started, David asked his adviser to remain beside him because he might need him when he greeted the guests – and he told him to ensure everything was perfect.

The Bad Adviser went to see Mr. LaRue and said, "I came to make sure that everything is perfect. We don't want any mistakes."

"Of course. As usual, we will do our job to perfection."

"Also, we will use only one trumpet when the King comes to gives his speech and we don't want a trumpet to welcome the Princess."

"That's strange!" said Mr. LaRue. "I'm not sure if that's wise because protocol doesn't say that!"

"The King and I have agreed on that because we think it's important that the King receives all the attention."

The guests started to arrive in the main hall and the servants welcomed them, all standing in one long line. Everything was perfect as they waited for King David to give his welcoming speech. The guards sounded a trumpet to notify the guests that the King had arrived and was about to give his speech. People stood up to show their respect to the King while Isabella waited for the second trumpet so she could descend the stairs. But no-one from the guard sounded their trumpet. She could hear her half-brother giving his speech and didn't understand what was happening – protocol dictated that they needed to use the trumpet to welcome the royal family.

While David had finished his speech, Isabella went to Mr. LaRue and angrily asked him why they hadn't used the trumpet to welcome her. "I felt embarrassed," she said, "and how come you broke protocol when you're the man who's supposed to observe it?"

"I beg your pardon, Your Highness. They told me not to use it."

"What do you mean by 'they?'?"

"The King's Adviser said that the King wanted it done that way."

Isabella couldn't understand why David wanted to do this and was unaware that in reality his adviser was behind it.

David went down to greet his guests while the Bad Adviser stood behind him, guiding him about what he should say to everyone. One of the businessmen from another kingdom, Mr. Edwards, came to greet David. David's father hadn't allowed him to conduct business in the kingdom because of his unethical practices – everyone knew that, including David.

"Your Majesty, let me use this moment to congratulate you on becoming king," Mr. Edwards said. "I wish you a glorious reign. I came today because I want to expand my business into your kingdom and I need your approval."

David looked him up and down and said, "Mr. Edwards, you know my father rejected your demands many times so why should

I accept them? You've used unethical practices for a long time. I won't let you bring them into my kingdom and I don't know why anyone sent you an invitation to my reception."

The Bad Adviser interrupted David and said, "Your Majesty, we need to see things from a different perspective. Mr. Edwards will make our economy much stronger and increase the employment rate which will make people feel happy."

"Adviser!" King David said. "It seems that you forget that *I* am the King and the only one who can accept or reject his offer."

Mr. Edwards decided to leave. As he went, the Bad Adviser told David that he needed to go to the kitchen and followed him.

The Bad Adviser called to the businessman, "Mr. Edwards! Wait! Stop!"

"If he wants to apologize, I won't accept it," said Mr. Edwards.

"If I convince the King to accept your offer, what will you give me?" asked the Bad Adviser.

"He's like his father," said Mr. Edwards, "and he won't ever accept my offer. I regret coming. I thought that because he was new, I might have had a chance to convince him."

The Bad Adviser told Mr. Edwards that he needed a large commission for every business deal he facilitated in the kingdom. Mr. Edwards accepted that because he knew that David wouldn't accept him. The Bad Adviser told Mr. Edwards to stay in town for a few days and he returned to David without raising suspicion. He walked with David through all the guests and waited until the reception had ended. He wanted to talk to him about Mr. Edwards but didn't get an opportunity.

The next morning, while the Bad Adviser was updating David about recent events, Isabella arrived and ask David if he'd ordered the guards not to welcome her with the trumpet, thereby breaking protocol. She said, "I don't know why you did that!"

"What? I don't understand!" David said. "And you can't address me as 'David' – I'm your King, so you need to address me as 'Your Majesty!'"

"Okay! Your Majesty, why did you order the guard to not welcome me as usual with the trumpet? I felt embarrassed!"

"But I don't order it!"

"If not you, then who did? Mr. LaRue said the order came from your adviser."

For the first time, David felt undermined in front of his sister, so he looked at the Bad Adviser as if to ask him if he'd given the order. The Bad Adviser said nervously. "Sorry, Your Majesty. Please forgive me. I forgot to mention it to you. The Professor taught me that the King should have all the attention at the first event he attends as King."

"I wanted to ask you where the Professor is," Isabella said. "It's been months since I've seen him and his family asked me about him. I didn't know what to say."

"Your Highness, the Professor is in prison," the Bad Adviser replied, "because he tried to kill the King."

"What? Wait!" said Isabella in shock. "I'm talking to David, not you. Why are you answering for him? I want to hear it from him."

"The Professor is a traitor, Isabella," David said.

"I don't believe you," said Isabella. "There's something you don't want to tell me but believe me I will find out." She then left.

"I hate Isabella!" said David. "She always thinks she's the smartest one in the room."

"Your Majesty, please don't worry about Isabella because she doesn't know how to govern the kingdom," the Bad Adviser said.

"I won't! Tell me what you wanted to say before Isabella arrived."

"I found a way that could enhance your image in front of the public so that you can show the citizens that you're like your father."

"Tell me!"

"It's to do with Mr. Edwards's offer."

"I won't accept his offer, you know that," said David.

"Yes, Your Majesty, but Mr. Edwards promised he will hire all of his employees locally which will enhance your image. I think you need to take action for your people even if the public thinks this isn't a wise decision."

"It isn't!"

"Your Majesty, I think we need to see the offer. Mr. Edwards will pay a large amount of taxes which will improve the kingdom's finances and this money can be allocated to help the poor."

David said, "Isabella doesn't know how to run the kingdom," and told his Adviser to accept Mr. Edwards's offer. The Bad Adviser sent for Mr. Edwards to tell him that the King had accepted his offer and remind him about his commission. Mr. Edwards gave the Bad Adviser a bag of money as a gesture of goodwill. It was the first time that the Bad Adviser had felt empowered for a while. He felt that he could do anything in the kingdom after a small word to David. Then he reminded Mr. Edwards that if he didn't send him his cut every month, he would see his business was closed down.

~ ~ ~

The more often Robert entered the shop to see Joseph standing there, the more he worried about Joseph one day taking his place. One day, he couldn't control his emotions anymore and challenged Joseph. This escalated to an argument and Robert punched him.

"So you think that you will steal my father's business?" Robert yelled

"Who said that? You – no-one else! It is your father's business and I'm only his employee."

"You liar, Joseph." Robert punched Joseph again and again.

The Antique Merchant came in and pulled Robert away from Joseph, telling him to leave. Robert was furious.

"Joseph, I'm sorry about my son's behavior and I hope you will accept my apologies," the Antique Merchant said.

"Sir, believe me, no hard feelings!"

"That's a relief."

A few weeks previously, while Robert was in the shop eating, the Antique Merchant had told Joseph that he wanted him to go to another city to sell two pieces to two different collectors. This conversation had made Robert extremely jealous and made him think that his father would give his business to Joseph instead of to him. Robert had decided to hide his jealousy, but the more he thought about it, the more he hated Joseph. He decided to act in front of his father as if he wanted to settle his problem with Joseph. He decided to apologize in front of his father and tell him that he was sorry about everything. Neither the Antique Merchant nor Joseph could believe that Robert was willing to admit his bad attitude.

~ ~ ~

The next day, Joseph woke up early and headed to the Antique Merchant to take his caravan and two antiques to sell it to the collectors. Before Joseph set off, he asked the Antique Merchant to give him tips about how he could close a deal with this kind of collector,

"Joseph, I am sending you to loyal customers of mine," said the Antique Merchant. "The antiques are so valuable that people sometimes can't estimate their true price. Remember that the price is based on what people think the thing is worth. I hope you can close these deals successfully."

Then the Antique Merchant and Robert said goodbye to Joseph. The Merchant asked Robert to go inside to talk with him and he told him that he was proud of his behavior because of what he'd done the day before. It was the first time the Antique Merchant had told his son that he was proud of him, which caused Robert to say in shock, "Really? Father!"

"Robert, you're my only son and I want you to work with me in the shop. The reason I didn't let you to work with me before is because you hadn't given yourself chance to change your behavior or develop some self-esteem."

"Father! I'm so happy because I know I can work beside you."

"You can start your job tomorrow."

It was a lovely moment of father and his son talking without anything between them, but Robert didn't reveal that the flame of jealousy toward Joseph was still within him.

~ ~ ~

After a few hours, Joseph had arrived at the city where the collectors lived. He stopped a local for directions saying, "Good morning. Could you direct me to the house of Mr. William Bates?"

"Well, you can go that way," the man said pointing, "and then turn left."

"Thank you, sir. Have a nice day."

When he arrived he knocked on the door which was opened by a servant who asked him to wait until the collector arrived. Mr. Bates, a wealthy English antique collector, soon appeared and greeted Joseph. They sat together and chatted. Mr. Bates told Joseph about his adventures and how he liked to collect antiques from all around the world. He'd traveled to many countries, from Asia to Africa. Joseph saw that his house was full of antiques and the collector showed him many of them, which bored Joseph but he kept that to himself. Finally, they sat on one of the couches and started to talk business.

"I see that the Antique Merchant doesn't want to waste his time coming himself," Mr. Bates said, "and he's sent a young man to sell his antiques. What do you have for me today?"

Joseph showed him both of the antiques, a vase from the Han dynasty and a painted bowl from the Yuan dynasty, and said, "Sir, choose what you want."

"I can't choose! How much would it cost me for both of them?"

"Sorry, sir, you can't buy both. I came to sell you only one piece because after I leave you I'm going to see another collector to sell him the other piece. I've been instructed to sell one piece to each customer."

At that moment Joseph remembered that the Antique Merchant hadn't told him what price he should sell the pieces for, but he remembered his advice which was that the price was based on perceived value. His strategy was to see what the collector thought the piece was worth. Mr. Bates chose the bowl and started to inspect it closely. He asked his servant to also check it and they spent a while checking the piece.

"I never thought the Antique Merchant would send a young man like you," said Mr. Bates. "Now I've evaluated it, I think I can pay five hundred coins for it."

"So sir, do you think that I will sell it for five hundred coins?"

"Mmm, maybe for five hundred and fifty coins?"

"Sir, do you think I will sell it for five hundred and fifty coins?"

"Yes, I think five hundred and fifty coins is a fair price."

"Sir, we have a deal. Congratulations!"

The collector gave Joseph his payment and before he left asked him about the real value of this antique. Joseph said: "Sir, believe me, I don't know. If I knew, I'd tell you, but what I know for sure is that paid what you think is a fair price."

Joseph took the money and asked the servant for directions to the second collector's house. When he arrived there, he knocked on the door, and the second collector opened the door himself. He welcomed Joseph and asked him to take a seat. This collector was a young man called Mr. Franceschini and he was a wealthy Italian antique collector. Joseph told him that he'd been with another collector before coming to him. The collector asked Joseph to show him the vase and he examined it. He told Joseph he liked it and said, "How much it will cost me?"

"Whatever you think is a fair price. I'll accept it."

The second collector thought for a moment and said, "A hundred coins!"

"Sir, do you think that I will sell it for a hundred coins?"

"Yes, I think it is a fair price for this piece due to the quality and the date it was created which is on the bottom of the vase."

Joseph took the money and returned to his caravan, heading to the city. In the late afternoon, he arrived back at the shop. The Antique Merchant was waiting for him and Joseph told him he had sold both pieces. He said, "I spent a lot of time with the first collector but the second one seemed to know to value the vase. I was wondering why you didn't tell me what price I should accept?"

"I wanted you to experience the tip that I gave it to you," the Merchant said.

"Sir, I trust whatever advice you give me because you have a lot of experience."

"That wasn't advice, but now I am going to give you advice. The reason I gave you that tip is that I wanted you to experience and test the tip yourself and to teach you a lesson."

"I'm a good listener!" Joseph replied.

"When you sell something you should be aware of the buyer's mindset because everyone looks at an antique from their own point of view. For example, we have premium profit with the first collector and lose out with the second collector, but we can cover the loss because the first collector overvalued the antique."

"I don't understand how this is related to the advice that you will give me."

"Everyone on this planet has a key," the Antique Merchant said. "If you know that key, you can sell anything to them. The first collector is wealthy and likes to collect antiques because he likes to own them, but the second one is a collector who wants to sell the antique in the future and that's why he knew the best price to offer."

Robert saw his father talking to Joseph and how he was happy because he had sold the antiques for a good price – jealousy was killing him from the inside. He wanted to do something. Robert felt that Joseph a threat and that made him feel insecure and he was becoming more paranoid day by day. He'd got to a point where he was willing to do anything to harm Joseph, forgetting that his father had given him a chance to work in the shop. Robert hid his jealousy and went to congratulate Joseph. The Antique Merchant was happy that they could work together as a team.

A few weeks later, while Joseph and Robert were working together at the shop, the Antique Merchant came over to them and said, "I'm going out of town for three days and I want both of you to be in charge while I'm gone."

That afternoon, Joseph and Robert greeted every customer who entered the shop. At the end of the day, Joseph was happy because now he could work with Robert in harmony after their long conflict.

On the second day, Joseph arrived at the shop to see Robert was waiting there. "You're here, Joseph," said Robert. "I need you to cover for me because I'm going to see one of my friends. His house is out of town so I expect to return after two days – the day my father's back."

Joseph told him that he would take charge that day and the next and Robert left. When the sun started to go down, Joseph was checking the inventory and he heard people screaming loudly, "Fire! Fire!"

Joseph panicked. He could smell something burning and when he left the storeroom, he saw that the whole shop was ablaze.

A guard said, "The antique shop is on fire."

A citizen who knew the Antique Merchant called out, "I think the Antique Merchant is in there!"

Another citizen shouted, "We need water!" and another yelled, "Water! Water!"

All the neighbors, guards, and people who were walking around came to help the person who is inside the shop, thinking it was the Antique Merchant. After a few hours, the fire had destroyed the property and all the antiques. The guard investigated the fire, deciding it was arson and the only suspect was Joseph. They sent him to prison so he could be judged the next day.

In the prison, the guard questioned him, and the investigator said, "What's your connection with the Antique Merchant?"

"I work for him, sir."

"Where is the Antique Merchant?"

"He's out of town."

"So you were alone?" asked the investigator.

"No, sir. The Antique Merchant assigned me and his son Robert responsibility for the shop while he's out of town."

"Where's Robert?"

"Yesterday he told me that he wanted to leave town to visit a friend. So I took charge of the stall alone," said Joseph.

"You're the only suspect, and there is no proof that you didn't commit arson."

"But sir, I didn't do it!" exclaimed Joseph. "I'm innocent!"

"Young man, if you have proof of this, give it to me now. Crimes such as arson, petty theft, attacking royal officials, stealing crops, and rebellion are serious crimes that law enforcement doesn't take lightly."

"Why would I want to commit arson in the place I work?"

"I'm not the judge," said the investigator. "Tomorrow you will go to the courthouse."

NICE ORDEAL

They took him to a cell located in the town prison. It was very small, dusty, and dirty, as well as filled with rats. Joseph was scared of going to prison for the second time. It was the middle of the night and Joseph couldn't sleep because he couldn't stop thinking about what had happened. *Surely no-one would harm the Antique Merchant? Was it a coincidence? Who would benefit from burning down the Antique Merchant's shop while he was out of town?*

When the sun started to rise, the guard came to escort him to the Judge. They put cuffs on his hands and feet and took him to the court where the Judge was waiting for him. The guard asked the public to stand up because the Judge had arrived and Joseph was the first case.

The Judge said, "In the name of the King of Ostax, and with the authority he gave me, I am here to give judgment on the case that a young man called Joseph committed arson in the Antique Merchant's shop. After reviewing the case, we could see that there is no suspect except Joseph who was working in the stall that night. In fact, we must consider the rights of the kingdom before seeing what the collateral damage is – in this case, the Antique Merchant's shop. Arson is a serious crime that could harm our community and citizens and destabilize our security. It is the right of the kingdom to punish those who did it and to compensate the Antique Merchant. Therefore, I sentence the defendant Joseph to five years in prison."

Joseph couldn't believe what had happened. For a moment, he felt paralyzed and he started to lose control of his emotions because of that adjudication. The guards put handcuffs back onto Joseph and took him to the caravan heading to the prison. On the way, Joseph was very sad because it was the second time he was going to prison for something he hadn't done. In the caravan he was with the other criminals. He felt frightened and remained silent until they arrived at the prison.

The caravan stopped at the prison and the guard sent Joseph to his cell. This prison was different from the first one because in this prison the prisoners could mix with each other. The cell he was supposed to be in was a big cell that could fit twelve people at the same time. The guard showed him his bed and told him that in the afternoon there was a break when the prisoners could talk to each other in the gardens located at the prison. It was a nightmare for him to think of these criminals sharing the same cell with him, especially when he remembered the cell that he'd shared with the Professor. Joseph recalled one of the principles that the Professor had taught him – that he should see his circumstances as preparation for what would come next, in this case, his rightful inheritance. Thinking about this possibility made Joseph feel less stressed so he started to ask himself questions, including *How will these circumstances help me move forward toward achieving my purpose? What do I need to learn in this step?*

The guard said in a loud voice, "Break, break, break."

This was the sign that the prisoners were allowed to go out for fresh air. Joseph walked into the gardens while everyone gazed at him, knowing from his countenance and bearing that this person would never commit a crime. Joseph walked a little and then sat in the corner, trying to adapt to his new circumstances with his freedom denied him for the second time in his life.

Stealthily, someone came over to him pointing a stick in his face as if it were a weapon.

The stranger's actions freaked Joseph out. The man said, "Hey, you. Why didn't you stand up to respect the King?"

"What? What king? I don't understand," Joseph said uncertainly.

The stranger, pointing at nothing. "You don't see him? That's strange. Everyone can see the King except you."

Joseph figured out that the stranger was delusional so he decided to indulge him and said, "I see him now! How are you, Your Majesty?" Then he whispered to the stranger, "Can he hear me?"

"Of course he heard you, he's the King. He likes me to tell you what he's saying." He told Joseph to move closer which he did and said, "The King's a shy person! The King told me to ask you about your name. What's your name?"

"My name is Joseph. What's yours?"

"Wait a second. Let me get permission from the King." He paused and added, "He's given me permission. My name is Wolfgang."

Joseph and Wolfgang talked throughout the break, talking about his imaginary friend, the imaginary king. Joseph was happy because he had a new friend to talk to and stop him from feeling bored in prison, even though Wolfgang was delusional. For a moment he felt that they had a special connection that made Joseph remember his friend Albert.

The guards told the prisoners that break was over and they needed to go back inside.

~ ~ ~

The Antique Merchant arrived back in the city and headed straight to his shop because he'd heard the news that it had been burned down. When he got there, he saw Robert on the ground crying. Jealousy was killing Robert and he couldn't see anything in front of him; it made him blind and he hadn't realized that his jealousy would harm him and his father. The Antique Merchant knew immediately that his only son had burned down the shop, not Joseph, so he went to the guard, saying, "I think Joseph is innocent. I don't want to press charges against him."

"I'm sorry, sir. It isn't about you anymore! It is the kingdom's right and arson is a serious crime."

~   ~   ~

The Bad Adviser hadn't told David that he had a meeting with the Royal Council. When the meeting began, the royal consul noticed the King's absence and sent a message sent to the Bad Adviser that they needed the King to attend. The Bad Adviser had expected this and he went to David and said, "Your Majesty, the Royal Council is having a meeting and they've been waiting for you for a while."

"I didn't know the Royal Council was holding a meeting today!" David replied. "I haven't prepared myself for a meeting! I don't think I want to go. You go on my behalf. I know that you will represent me well. You always serve me in the best way and have resolved many problems for me. Without you, I can't run the kingdom!"

"Your wish is my command, Your Majesty."

This was a win for the Bad Adviser now King David trusted him more – it meant he could now talk on behalf of the King, in the name of the King. He went to the Royal Council meeting with his own guard but the other members didn't stand up for him because they were waiting for the King to arrive and open the meeting. The Bad Adviser took the chair that the King was supposed to sit in and opened the meeting, saying "From now on, I will attend Royal Council meetings instead of the King, and will speak as the King." The members of the Royal Council looked at each other in wonder because such a thing had never happened before.

The Bad Adviser pushed all the decisions in a way that would benefit him in the future, not in the best interests of the kingdom or even David. Day after day, the Bad Adviser became more tyrannical, not allowing anyone to disagree with him – should they try to do so, he reminded them that he was the King's adviser. They couldn't do anything because no-one was allowed to disagree with the King. No-one was even allowed to meet with the King unless the Bad Adviser approved it. The Bad Adviser isolated David from everything to do with the public, the Royal Council, and his half-sister Isabella.

~   ~   ~

Back at the prison, Joseph was lying in bed thinking deeply about everyone he knew, from his foster family, the Baker and Karma to the Professor and the Antique Merchant. He mused on what would come next and how he would get back his throne, and clear his reputation. *How could he convince them that the King had another living son?*

The prisoner who was sitting beside his bed saw Joseph was awake and said, "The first night in prison is always the most dismal but believe me in time you'll be okay. You need to have faith."

"Faith!" said Joseph. "That's the only thing I have now and I will have in the future."

At the end of the first week, Joseph had spoken to no-one except to Wolfgang during the lunch break. But he noticed a huge man who was the cause of much fear because no-one could touch him and he was a bully. Everyone in the prison tried to avoid him because he was a frightening person. Even the guards tried to be polite to him.

Joseph said to Wolfgang while pointing to the huge man, "Who is that? And why does he bully everyone in the prison?"

"That's Wally. No one can touch him, and the King told me he lives in the cell alone and sometimes he eats people! Don't talk to him."

Joseph noticed that Wally abused everyone in the prison. He took their lunch, picked fights with them, and stole their blankets. Joseph decided to ignore him and avoid any contact with him. One day, when he was sitting with Wolfgang during the lunch break, Wally came over and said to Wolfgang in front of Joseph to that he was going to take his lunch. Wolfgang didn't do anything, and Wally threw him to the floor. Joseph decided to be brave and stand up to Wally. Although Wally was stronger and tougher than him, he couldn't watch Wally bully his friend Wolfgang and do nothing. For the first time, the prisoners saw someone confront Wally and say "no" to him.

While Wolfgang was on the ground, Joseph stood in front of Wally and said, "Wally, I won't allow you to bully my friend." All the prisoners started to watch them. Wally angrily kicked Joseph which caused Joseph to fall to the ground but he immediately stood up again. Wally kicked Joseph ten more times and each time Joseph stood up and confronted him again.

Wolfgang decided to stand up with Joseph, knowing that Wally would attack them. Wally threw both Joseph and Wolfgang to the ground and they stood up again every time. Everyone in the prison had been watching and another prisoner felt brave and decided to join them. Now there were three prisoners standing up to Wally and this made him even more aggressive. Then more prisoners came to join them – three, six, nine… Wally lost control and tried to attack them all, but he realized he couldn't prevail, so he gave up. Wally, who spread fear and bullied everyone, had given up and ran to sit in the corner. He would never bully anyone again. The prisoners started to call Joseph's name, and his reputation started to increase in the prison.

But although the prisoners could now walk around the prison peacefully knowing that Wally wouldn't attack them, Joseph wasn't happy because when he stood up in front of Wally, he didn't see a brave huge man. He saw in Wally's eyes pain and suffering. So Joseph in front of everyone went to Wally, walked to the corner to talk to him, knowing that at any moment Wally could fly into a rage and hurt him.

Joseph trusted his instincts and said, "Hi Wally, it's me, Joseph!"

Wally stuttered, "Wha–, wha–, what do you want?"

"It's okay, Wally!" said Joseph.

Until lunch break was over, Joseph and Wally talked. It was the first time that Wally had spoken to anyone in the prison. Joseph could see that there was a person inside Wally who had been suffocating for a while because of his huge body. It was a memorable moment when people saw Wally laugh for the first time, Wally made a pinky swear with his huge hand to promise

Joseph that he wouldn't harm anyone. He'd only needed someone to accept him. After he talked to him, Joseph realized that Wally was ashamed of his huge body and being different from others, but after talking to Joseph, Wally became a new, helpful, and caring man, a decent man who helped the prisoners trying to stop the cycle of bullying.

~   ~   ~

General Graham had heard that the percentage of unethical businesses had been increasing for a while and was higher than it had been when the old King was alive. He went to the Bad Adviser to update the King, but the Bad Adviser tried to kill the story by telling him that he would pass it onto the King but he didn't do so. The Bad Adviser had started to give approval on behalf of the King to unethical traders, allowing them to export their businesses to the kingdom without telling the King. He took bribes from any businessman who offered one in exchange for letting them sell their merchandise in the kingdom. The Bad Adviser was becoming richer and more powerful. Everyone had noticed, but they couldn't do anything because no-one could talk to the King unless the Bad Adviser approved.

The Bad Adviser also started to abuse his authority with the castle employees. He fired one, then terminated another. He realized by the way the Chief of Guards had started to ask a lot of questions that he was an obstacle, but he couldn't fire him because the Bad Adviser didn't have any power when it came to matters related to the guards. So The Bad Adviser went to David and said,

"Your Majesty, it seems that General Graham isn't performing well lately and I think it would be a good idea to replace him."

"But if I were to replace him, who do you think would be a good replacement?" David asked. "No-one has experience like his!"

"Maybe we could demote the General and make him the Deputy of the Guard, and then you can choose someone you trust to be the new Chief of Guard."

"Like who?"

"You're the King, Your Majesty, but it's important to choose someone that you trust with your life." The Bad Adviser was telling David that he was the best candidate to be the Chief of Guard, but he was waiting for it to come from David so no-one could disagree with him.

"What about you? I think you'd be a good Chief of Guard," said David.

"Who? Me?" exclaimed the Bad Adviser. "Chief of Guard? I'm not fit for that position." Then he lowered his head and said, "Maybe if the present Chief of Guard became my assistant so I could get benefit from his experience..."

Once the Bad Adviser was the Chief of Guard as well the King's Adviser he became the most powerful person in the kingdom and could do anything in the name of the King while David was immersing himself in childish pleasures.

~ ~ ~

The leader of the gang in Zelaar wanted payment for the services he'd given the Bad Adviser so he sent a message to the Bad Adviser telling him that he wanted to talk to him. After a few days, the Bad Adviser went to see the gang leader covertly because he didn't want anyone to ask why the King's Adviser was with one of the most dangerous criminals in the kingdom. The gang leader told the Bad Adviser that his brother was in prison and he wanted help to get him out. The Bad Adviser agreed believing that the brother was in prison in the kingdom of Zelaar.

"No," said the gang leader when he realized the misunderstanding. "My brother is in prison in the Kingdom of Ostax. If he was in prison here, it would be easy for me to help him to escape."

"You're insane!" said the Bad Adviser. "How can I help a prisoner escape on soil where I don't have any influence?"

"I thought of a solution but it needs you to push it because no-one can do it except the King."

The Bad Adviser laughed. "Who is the King? I'm the real King in Zelaar. Please don't mention the name of that child called David."

The gang leader looked him in the eyes and said, "So you can do it?"

"What's your solution?"

"The only way to bring my brother back from the Kingdom of Ostax is for King David to arrange a prisoner exchange between the Kingdom of Zelaar and the Kingdom of Ostax. That would make my task much easier. And it will improve King David's image because it will show that he cares about his people inside and outside the kingdom. Plus, you'll get credit for this suggestion, which means the King will trust you even more!"

"Brilliant idea!" said the Bad Adviser. "Give me some time so I can think about how to do it. And after this I'm no longer in your debt. Is that clear?"

"As you wish."

The Bad Adviser went to David while he was sitting on his throne, feeling lonely.

"Good afternoon, Your Majesty. How are you?"

"I'm doing fine, but I am feeling bored because I do nothing – I never expected that."

"Your Majesty," said the Bad Adviser said, "You don't need to do anything. You're the King. Ask and you will receive. We're here to serve you, working all day and night to enhance your image and help you build a legacy as King that history will not ignore."

"Get to the point," said David.

"Your Majesty, I have an idea that will help us to enhance your image in front of the public and cut the cost of the prison budget. Also, you need to show that you care about your citizens inside and outside the kingdom."

"Outside the kingdom?"

The Bad Adviser explained the idea of a prisoner exchange with another kingdom, starting with the nearest, the Kingdom of

Ostax, and saying how it would benefit a lot of families enabling them to visit their fathers or brothers. David liked the idea and asked his Adviser to write a letter he could send to the King of Ostax personally.

~ ~ ~

Everyone had started to talk to Joseph and he figured out that none of the prisoners were able to read or write so he decided to teach them everything he knew. Day by day, the number who wanted to attend Joseph's classes started to increase. Joseph was happy because now he could have an impact on people's lives in prison which made him feel that he had a purpose. After a few months, the illiteracy rate started to drop, people became more educated and started to engage in debate. The prisoners started to demand books instead of visiting time, which made the Prison Governor respect and appreciate Joseph even more.

During one lunch break when Joseph had finished his teaching, Wolfgang came to talk with him. He said, "The King told me to tell you that you're a good man."

"Thank you," Joseph replied, "and please tell the King that I thank him for seeing that in me."

"And he told me to ask you if you have a family outside the prison."

"I have two families. The family who raised me and my birth family."

"Really? How come you have two families?"

Joseph started to tell him his story assuming that Wolfgang wouldn't believe him, but the story captivated Wolfgang and he told Joseph him that when he became king, he needed to visit him in prison. Wolfgang added, "You're really King? Does that you have a big plate of dessert?"

Joseph laughed. "I'm not yet a king, but soon I will be. About the big plates of dessert – I'm not sure. If I do get a big plate, I'll give you some."

"Promise?"

"Promise. What about you? Do you have a family? Tell me your story. Why are you in prison?"

"A long time ago, my father passed away," Wolfgang said, "and my mother is alive but lately she's been sick."

"In what way?"

"She can't remember who I am. She forgets that she has a living son and I used to tell her the story of the king who will end all evil in the world."

"Is this the same king you talk to?"

"Yes," said Wolfgang. "The king I talked to helps me remember my mother. The more I immerse myself in my imagination, the more I remember my mother. Until… "

"Until what?"

"One day, people suddenly came to our house and killed my mother and robbed us of her jewelry. The guard accused me of killing my mother. I don't remember if it's true or not."

KING UNDERCOVER

ing David sent a letter with his adviser to the King of Ostax telling him about his offer of exchanging prisoners between the kingdoms. The King of Ostax ordered the Prison Governor to separate prisoners from the Kingdom of Zelaar so they could do the exchange.

The Prison Governor came to the prisoners during the lunch break and asked his guard to bring him the prisoners from Zelaar. They gathered in his office, and he told them about the exchange and that within one week they would be in the Zelaar prison. This made Joseph panic because if he arrived at that prison, the guard would recognize him as someone who'd escaped.

After the meeting, Wolfgang said, "Joseph, the King asked me to ask you why you're upset."

"They're going to do an exchange between prisoners!" Joseph replied in a sad voice.

"But this is supposed to be good news! Isn't it?"

Joseph explained that he'd escaped from the prison with the help of one of the prison guards and that if he went back, he couldn't escape again and he wouldn't be able to reclaim his throne.

Wolfgang lowered his head and said shyly. "Joseph, the King told me – sorry not the King – *I* want to tell you that I'm glad I got to know you. You're a decent man, and you had a good impact on the prison. I hope that one day you'll be king." It was the first time Wolfgang had spoken to Joseph as Wolfgang and not through his imaginary king, which made Joseph feel happy. Joseph reminded him that if he became king, he would visit Wolfgang and bring a big plate of dessert.

~ ~ ~

Isabella saw the assistant of the Chief of Guards and called him over to talk to him.

"Your Highness, is there are any help I give you?" asked General Graham.

"I need an explanation about what's happening in the kingdom," Isabella said. "You served my father and my grandfather before him. You know things that others don't. Tell me what's happening right now."

General Graham explained that David had sent the Professor to prison the night of her father's ceremony when he was greeting guests in the royal main hall. He said he also believed that David was behind killing the King, the riots, and accusing twenty-one innocent people. General Graham thought it was with the help of the Bad Adviser who planned everything. "And now he's demoted me and become the Chief of Guard," he concluded.

Isabella was furious because she hadn't expected her half-brother to do such things.

"Do you want anything more, your Highness?" General Graham asked. "Because now I need to fetch the prisoners from the Kingdom of Ostax because the King wants to do an exchange between the two kingdoms."

"I think I should go with you," Isabella said, "because I want an assistant who can help me in the castle while the Professor is in prison."

"But, Your Highness, these are serious criminals!"

"Well, you told me that you've thrown twenty-one innocent people into prison so some might be innocent. Isn't that possible?"

"But I will choose for you, Your Highness."

General Graham and Isabella went to Ostax prison to choose a prisoner. The Prison Governor greeted them and told them that the prisoners were ready for the exchange, and General Graham told him that the Princess wanted to choose someone to be her servant.

"Anyone specific, Your Highness?" asked the Prison Governor.

"Someone who can be fit to work with me in the castle as assistant."

All the prisoners were standing in a row. The Prison Governor said to them, "Now, you are all going to set off in the caravans to Zelaar prison's where your families are. This will make your families' lives easier because they will be able to visit you. Also, Princess Isabella of Zelaar will choose one of you to serve her in the castle."

All the prisoners wanted to work in the castle instead of completing their service in the prison, but no-one nominates himself. All the prisoners looked to one prison in the row – Joseph, Everyone thought that Joseph deserved this opportunity because he was a decent man. Isabella saw the prisoners gazing at Joseph and asked the Prison Governor why they did this.

The Prison Governor said, "Well, Your Highness, they are gazing at the best candidate to work with you. I was going to choose him. Joseph is a good man who has helped the prisoners learn how to read and write."

General Graham looked at Joseph and felt that he'd seen him before, but he wasn't sure where. For a moment, he looked at Joseph suspiciously. Joseph felt fearful, but he tried not to show that he was nervous. He set off in the royal caravan with Isabella. General Graham had told her that he wanted to join with her for her safety, but she'd insisted on being alone with Joseph, As he would work with her in the castle, she wanted to talk to him while they were traveling to the castle.

"So you are Joseph!" Isabella said.

Joseph lowered his head and said, "Yes, Your Highness. Thank you for choosing me. I promise I will do my work well."

"Believe me, I didn't choose you. Your friends and the Prison Governor urged me to choose you." she laughed and said, "Maybe it's fate."

Joseph looked out of the window and said, "Fate, it may be fate."

Isabella stared at him closely and said, "Do I know you? I think I've seen you before."

"Your Highness, it's a big world. Maybe you saw someone who looks like me?"

"Maybe! So why were you in prison?"

"Fate, Your Highness. It's a long story."

"I won't judge you for your past," said Isabella. "Your reputation was why I chose you. I expect you not to betray my trust – that's the most important thing for me."

They arrived at the castle and Isabella asked one of her servants to show Joseph his room. Joseph sat on his bed and wondered when everything would end and he would become king. Then one of the servants arrived saying, "This is your food. Please make yourself at home. Once you've finished you need to go to the Princess."

When Joseph went to Isabella she said, "I hope you liked your room?"

Joseph said politely, "I am so thankful for this opportunity and I liked the room that you gave me – it's completely different from the prison!"

"They told me that you're a good teacher. Is that true?" Isabella asked.

"Yes, Your Highness. In my free time I taught the prisoners many subjects"

"I think I'll need you because the Professor isn't here – oh, of course, you don't know the Professor. I don't know why I said that. It's a long story, and I miss him. I think you can take his place as my teacher."

Isabella dismissed Joseph and he went to his room and started to ask himself many questions: Do *I need to tell my story to my sister Isabella? What should I do now?* Then he decided, *I need to lie low so no-one will recognize me!*

General Graham came to see Joseph and asked, "Do you like your room?"

"Yes sir, I like it. It's far better than prison!"

"Of course it's better than prison!" said General Graham. "I came to tell you that I'm watching you. I've seen you before but have forgotten where and when."

Joseph was panicking because he didn't want General Graham to remember he was the person who he'd forced to plead guilty to the riots.

After a few months Joseph was doing well at his job of servant to Isabella and she'd started to trust him. On the other hand, King David was feeling bored because he wasn't doing anything in the kingdom but was letting the Bad Adviser do all the work. He called his adviser to have a talk with him and said, "I feel bored and I want to meet people. I want to be a real king like my father."

"Your Majesty, it isn't safe to go outside because a lot of people hate you. Remember we've had a lot of riots over the last few months."

"But I'm King, and I want to go!" David replied angrily.

"Your Majesty, I suggest you don't go out in public, but I think I've had a good idea for you."

"What?"

"Your best option in the circumstances is to host a reception. You can invite all the ministers, politicians, and artists. This will be safer for you because we can control the reception, but in public someone could attack you."

Straight after their conversation, the Bad Adviser told Mr. LaRue to prepare for the King's reception and send invitations in the name of the King.

On the day of the reception, Isabella was preparing to attend. Joseph, dressed as a servant, asked her if she needed anything.

"Why are you dressed like that?" Isabella asked. "Today we have an important reception and you need to be well dressed."

"I don't have any other clothes, Your Highness, and I don't know if it's appropriate for me to attend the King's ceremony."

"Believe me, you'll enjoy it. I trust you because from today you're my adviser. A lot of people will attend the ceremony and I need you beside me."

Joseph went to his room and Isabella sent someone to fetch Joseph some elegant clothes. Isabella asked Joseph him to go to her before the ceremony started because she wanted him to walk with her while she descended the stairs when the guard welcomed her by sounding their trumpets.

All the servants in the castle were waiting for the King's guests. When it was early evening, the guests had begun to arrive and the staff stood in a row to greet them. When almost all the guests had arrived, the royal guards sounded their trumpets to announce the King's arrival. Then one of the guards said loudly, "Please stand up to welcome our King."

The King appeared on the balcony and waved to his guests. The second trumpet welcomed Isabella and she descended the stairs with Joseph walking beside her – no-one could recognize him because he was too far away.

With the statesmen, members of the Royal Council, and other people close to the royal family there, the main kitchen couldn't accommodate all the guests so they brought in outside contractors from butchers and bakeries that had supplied the castle for years. Mr. LaRue sent a message to the Baker to send one of his employees to help serve the bread he was supplying. That was Hither.

Princess Isabella started to greet everyone and shake their hands and Joseph was ready for anything that Isabella asked him about. He had learned many things about politics because Isabella had told what was happening in the kingdom. And she had taken his advice on many matters. Over the last few months, she'd come to trust him more, and she was pleased that she'd made Joseph her adviser. Isabella was talking to one of the guests when she noticed a woman serving bread, so she called the servant over to offer the person who she was talking to some bread as hospitality. When the woman came closer Joseph saw it was Hither and tried to avoid eye contact with her.

Isabella said to the guest, "Your Excellency, let me offer you some delicious bread from one of the oldest bakeries in town."

"Thank you, Your Highness."

Isabella said, "Joseph! You should try some."

At that moment Hither looked at Joseph and recognized him. Joseph tried to tell Hither through his eyes: *Pretend you don't know me.* Isabella saw them look at each other and asked Joseph if he knew her. Joseph said that he'd simply lost focus for a moment.

Hither moved away to serve other guests, watching Joseph from a distance, wondering what had happened to him, and Joseph pretended that he didn't know her. Isabella greeted more guests and called, "Joseph! Come here. I want you to meet someone."

"Yes, Your Highness," Joseph said and he could hardly breathe because this guest was the Judge.

Isabella was saying to the Judge, "Your honor, let me introduce you to my new adviser."

"Joseph!" said the Judge in shock.

"Do you know each other?" Isabella asked.

"No!" said the Judge nervously. "His reputation comes before him. I heard he is a good man."

"It's my honor to meet you, Your Honor," Joseph said.

The Judge was clever in realizing that Joseph didn't want anyone to know his identity. Joseph felt safe now no-one could figure out who he was, but now he'd seen Hither, he needed her to bring the sword from the bakery shop. Joseph excused himself from Isabella for a moment and signaled Hither. They went outside to talk privately.

"Joseph! Tell me what's happening," Hither said. "Why aren't you in prison? The wheat Supplier told my father that you were in prison. Why are you with the Princess?"

"It's a long story," Joseph responded, "but since you're here I need you to go to the bakery now and bring the sword for me because once the reception is over you won't be allowed to come inside. I can't go out in public to bring the sword from the bakery because they will figure out that I'm Joseph who they think was responsible for the riots."

"But if I go now, who will serve the bread? They'll be suspicious if I'm not there."

"Well, I did it once before, and I think that I can do it again," Joseph said. "When you return to the castle, meet me here, outside, so no-one will see us."

Hither ran to the bakery to bring the sword while Joseph took her place serving the bread to guests. Isabella noticed and asked why he was serving the bread

"I'm being a gentleman," Joseph said. "The woman who served the bread told me that she wanted to do something and asked me for help. I couldn't refuse her!"

Isabella laughed. "You're crazy!"

~ ~ ~

Hither arrived at the bakery and asked her father, "Where's Joseph's sword?"

"I don't understand. Why do you need it now?"

"Joseph's here!"

"Here? Is he with you right now?"

"No, he's in the castle," said Hither.

"What brings him to the castle?"

"I'll tell you later, but now I need the sword because Joseph needs it and I need to return to the King's reception."

Hither took the sword and covered it so no-one would see what she was carrying and so she could pass the checkpoint outside the castle, pretending that she'd left something behind in the bakery.

~ ~ ~

Hither went to the place where she'd spoken to Joseph and found him waiting there. "Did you bring it?" he asked.

"Yes, take it. I need to go inside so no-one will wonder why a servant is outside!"

Joseph took the sword and said, "You've saved my life, Hither."

General Graham had wondered why Joseph had been serving the bread and had followed him. He saw two people in the dark talking to each other but didn't know who they were, so he said loudly, "Who's there?" By the time he arrived, one of them had run away.

General Graham said to Hither, "Who you were talking to?"

"I wasn't talking to anyone, sir."

"I think I saw you with someone," General Graham replied.

"No sir, I was tired and went outside for fresh air."

General Graham went back inside.

~ ~ ~

Joseph quickly went to his room and put the sword under his bed before returning to the reception to be near Isabella. Once he'd left, General Graham went to Joseph's room because he was sure that he'd seen Joseph with the woman who served the bread. He searched Joseph's room and found the sword.

The ceremony had finished, and Joseph returned to his room to find General Graham, waiting for him. He was full of panic but the General bowed to him.

"Why are you bowing to me?" Joseph asked.

General Graham showed him the sword and said, "Because of this, Your Highness. I knew that one day you would return and I am sorry for treating you with suspicion."

General Graham then revealed that he'd been the loyal knight who Joseph's mother, the Queen, had sent with the sword and money to convince the farmer to take him. He told Joseph that he needed to claim his throne because the Bad Adviser was taking control from his half-brother and a lot of people were suffering because of his leadership.

Joseph said, "I have a plan and I will need your help, but we need to wait till I find the best moment to put it into action."

CHARADE

Nine months passed, and Isabella trusted only Joseph. Sometimes she asked for him simply to talk to him. She said that felt that they shared a connection that she couldn't explain. "Sometimes I feel as if I've known you for years," she said. "Sometimes I feel like you're my brother even though my mother only gave birth to one child – me."

Joseph responded and said: "Your Highness, you will never know."

"Joseph, I was thinking about something."

"What, Your Highness?"

"I was wondering if you could attend the Royal Council on my behalf," Isabella said. "What do you think?"

"It would be my pleasure, Your Highness."

Joseph hadn't expected that and he didn't want any contact with the Bad Adviser – he knew the Bad Adviser always attended Council meetings on behalf of the King. But Isabella sent notice to Mr. LaRue that she wanted Joseph to attend that afternoon's meeting on her behalf.

All the members of the Royal Council were present at the meeting and waited for the Bad Adviser to open it. Once he did, Joseph thought it was okay to offer his opinion because he represented Isabella so he stood up and shared an opinion on one of the matters that concerned him.

"Sorry? Who are you?" asked the Bad Adviser.

"I'm Joseph, Princess Isabella's Adviser."

"Since when has Isabella had an adviser? Why she didn't come? Why did she send you?"

One of the members sitting beside Joseph said, "Don't say anything!"

"What? Why?" said Joseph.

The man said in a low voice, "I'll tell you after the meeting."

After the meeting, Joseph asked the member who was beside him why he'd told him to not talk. "It's your first meeting, young man. We can't share our opinions because the King's adviser might harm us. He speaks on behalf of the King and in the name of the King. Believe me, we fear him more than we fear the King."

Joseph told Isabella what had happened and she told him that she knew about the situation but she couldn't do anything. At that moment, Joseph felt that he wanted to share his true story with her. "Isabella…" he started.

"What! Since when do you address me as Isabella?"

"I need to tell you something!" Joseph replied. "I'm your brother. Our mother, the Queen, gave birth to twins – a boy and a girl. The boy was me and the girl was you."

Joseph told her his story from the first time he'd seen the sword when he was eleven years old until the day she'd chosen him to work as her servant. He told her that he'd met the Professor in prison and spent time with him. Isabella didn't believe him until he showed her the sword and called General Graham to confirm his story.

Joseph, Isabella, and General Graham decided to work together to help Joseph claim his throne, but the Bad Adviser was such an obstacle for them that they needed to get rid of him. Also, they needed to crown Joseph in the old way, by gaining the support of the Royal Council while he held the sword in front of everyone in the royal main hall like his ancestors had done before him.

After two weeks, Joseph called Isabella and General Graham to share with them his plan and describe how they would execute it. Joseph told them that they needed to execute it at one of the King's receptions and they should make sure that all the members of the Royal Council were present, and they need to release the Professor from prison for the coronation.

"I will find the best moment. In a month's time, it will be the King's anniversary. That would be an ideal time," Isabella said.

"On that day I'll release the Professor from prison," General Graham said.

"What about you?" Isabella said to Joseph.

"It will be a surprise," said Joseph. "I'll contact an old friend who will help me."

On the day of the King's anniversary, everyone was sticking to their plan while Joseph was preparing a surprise – he didn't share this with General Graham or Isabella. This was one of the biggest receptions that the King had ever held and everyone was welcome to attend. everyone had worked for three whole nights to accommodate all the guests.

That afternoon people started to arrive. When almost all of the guests were present, the royal guards sounded their trumpets. Then one of the guards said loudly, "Please stand up to welcome our King."

King David arrived and waved at his guests with everyone standing to show their respect. Then, the second trumpet sounded to welcome Princess Isabella as she arrived with Joseph. On that day, Joseph was dressed like a king, someone born to be king.

Joseph's surprise was that he'd contacted his friend Thomas who worked in the circus to perform entertainment for the King's guests. With other members of the circus, he performed a play about the kingdom's folklore and narrated the relationship between the kingdom and the sword. The play described how a few centuries ago the area had been at war for seven years. Hundreds of thousands had died from starvation, war, and poverty until seven warriors got together to end the tragedy by uniting the people under one thing, under one king.

The seven warriors had sacrificed themselves to end the *Scorcharis Demoaris* curse and let the spirits choose one of them to take the throne for himself and his descendants. The warriors pledged allegiance by taking an oath that every king would pass this sword onto the future king, reminding them about the special power the sword had to help each future king by saying, "The sword will find, prepare, and guide the future king to find his rightful heir".

Everyone from the circus – from Thomas to the monkey – performed in the play. No-one suspected that this was the calm before the storm. Once it had ended, Joseph stood in front of the people attending the ceremony and said, "Dear Royal Council, a man who has lost his morals lost himself, and he who loses himself he will never win anything. People who stand by their ethics and morality might one day be upset if they lose everything, but they will never ever be upset for eternity because in the end, they are the winners. For centuries and generations, this kingdom gained its strength from the power of the sword, the power of ancestry, the power of the people. That's how tradition says that the future king should gain advocacy from the Royal Council and from the people."

Joseph gave the sign for General Graham to bring in the Professor and the guests were amazed. Then Joseph said loudly that he was the rightful king while the Professor and General Graham stood beside him. No-one could believe what was happening and the Bad Adviser shouted an order to the guards, "Arrest him!" Then he added, "He's a liar as are the Professor and the General."

The members of the Royal Council were watching what was happening and whispering to each other, "Is he the legal king?"

One of them said, "Let's wait and see."

Another said in a loud voice, "I know him. This person pleaded not guilty to causing the riots. He's a liar!"

The Judge stood up and said to everyone, "General Graham, when he was the Chief of Guard, ordered Joseph arrested because King David ordered him to do that." Then he went to stand beside the General. Joseph, the Professor, and Isabella joined them.

At that moment, Joseph pulled out the sword and held it high so everyone could see it. Now was the moment to prove to everyone that Joseph was the true king. The sword started to spark, releasing a light ball that flew all around the castle. This was a true spectacle and proof that Joseph was the king, the true king. The Royal Council fell to their knees and pledged allegiance to the King of Zelaar.

The guards rejected the order the Bad Adviser had given them to arrest Joseph, and Joseph ordered them to arrest the Bad Adviser. Everyone was happy because Joseph was now King, and Isabella was watching him with pride. Joseph noticed at that moment that both the Baker and Hither were present.

David took the opportunity to run away since Joseph hadn't ordered the guard to arrest him, and Joseph was taking the guests' attention. David sneaked outside and stole a horse and rode away. He felt shock, anger, envy, and jealousy because he had a half-brother who'd taken his throne from him.

Thomas went to Joseph and told him that he had a surprise for him. Joseph looked to the corner and saw that Thomas had invited his foster family and his best friend Albert.

"How did you do that?" Joseph asked Thomas. "And thank you. I never expected this."

"It's a small thing I do for a great friend like you," Thomas said, and he bowed and added, "Your Majesty."

Then Mariam came over to him and Joseph gave her the bracelet that she'd given him when he started his journey and called for the Professor. "Professor, I was wondering if I could give the title of Duchess to my foster sister, Mariam."

"You're the King and therefore you can do anything you desire," the Professor replied.

Joseph said, "Mariam, you always supported me and I promised to make you a duchess. Please kneel." He put his sword on Mariam's shoulder and said, "Now you are Duchess Mariam of Zelaar."

Mariam had never expected Joseph to remember his promise to make her a duchess; she hugged him and cried. Joseph started to weep because of seeing everyone surround and because now he was to be King. Everyone congratulated Joseph and he sat on the throne. He promoted General Graham to Chief of Guard and asked the Professor to be the King's Adviser.

~ ~ ~

A few days later Joseph his guards to travel to the north with him. When they were between the Kingdoms of Zelaar and Ostax, they saw the group of highwaymen that had taken his money and the horse that the Baker had given him. He demanded that they return the money and the horse to him immediately, which they did.

When Joseph arrived at the prison in the Kingdom of Ostax, the Prison Governor greeted him. Joseph entered the prison during the lunch break and everyone welcomed him except Wolfgang because he was sitting in the corner and didn't want to see or talk to anyone.

Joseph called in a loud voice, "Wolfgang!"

Wolfgang looked around and said, "Joseph! Joseph! Joseph's here! Joseph's here!"

Joseph gave an order to the guard who gave to Wolfgang what he'd promised him. Joseph said, "This is what I promised you. This is a big plate of dessert."

"You are the King. You are the King," said Wolfgang in a loud voice.

Joseph surprised Wolfgang with something more – a pardon from the King of Ostax. And before Joseph left the prison, he went to Wally, and saw that Wally had changed from being aggressive to being friendly. Wally was now a helpful man and Joseph spoke to the King so he would also be pardoned. The last thing Joseph did was when he got back to the Kingdom of Zelaar was to go to the prison to pardon his friend Richard who'd helped him escape.

~ ~ ~

Mr. Galvestone said to Lewis, his grandson, "Now, it's time for you to go home. We've finished the story of *Joseph and the Seven Swords.*"

Lewis and Patrick looked at each other and said, "Wow! What a story!"

"What did you learn from this story?" Mr. Galvestone asked.

"That everything is connected?" Claire said.

"You're correct, Claire. And what else?"

"To follow the signs?" Sophia asked.

"Why?" asked Mr. Galvestone.

"Because it will lead us toward your purpose!" Sophia said.

"Grandfather, why didn't Joseph marry Karma?" Charlotte asked. "Wasn't she his twin flame?"

"He perhaps hadn't found his twin flame yet," Mr. Galvestone answered, "but in time he will and he knows that what's meant to be is inevitable. Maybe it was meant to be, but not at that time"

Then he moved his head to look at the wall and the sword sparked.

To be continued.

About the Author

For author Faisal, the hero's journey begins off the page long before it manifests into a work of fiction. Deep within every heart lies a trove of hidden secrets, dangerous dreams, limiting beliefs, and endless potential. It is the storyteller's job to peel back those layers, one revelation at a time, until we finally grasp the truth that connects us all.

This search for wisdom has guided Faisal from his earliest days. As an underachieving teenager he spent much of his time lost in virtual gaming worlds, until a flash of enlightenment led him to see life through a new lens at age fifteen. From apathetic to inspired, he began attending courses, seminars, and workshops to discover his full potential and form intense connections with others intellectually and emotionally. Initially, Faisal found his community on a social network, where his commentary on politics and culture garnered tens of thousands of followers. He would soon after attract national attention as the youngest professional columnist in Kuwait.

Faisal's writing trajectory might have been steep, but it has also been far from easy. While studying on a scholarship in the US, he withdrew from his engineering degree program.

He gave himself the gift of a sabbatical year, leaving behind worldly distractions to explore the depths of introspection. When he emerged from his figurative chrysalis, mentally and spiritually transformed, he stepped into a new existence of joy, love, and inner peace.

This led to the birth of his debut fantasy novel, Joseph and the Seven Swords.

Faisal loves connecting with readers, so feel free to visit

www.Joetagonist.com.

JOETAGONIST ABOUT US

"An open book is a brain that speaks; closed, a friend that waits; forgotten, a soul that forgives; destroyed, a heart that cries". (Hindu proverb).

There are thousands of books that can become unique pieces of literature for you, books that will help you in bad moments and even become friends that will accompany you throughout your life. At Joetagonist, we don't believe that books are simply valuable, but that they are pure value.

That's why we create value.

We create books, stories, tales. But most of all, we create valuable experiences in each of our readers' lives. Our primary value is, indeed, creating value.

Therefore, Joetagonist is a leading creative project that seeks to revolutionize the publishing industry by making an iconic and inspiring thousands of people around the globe. Our challenge is not to sell, but to find the convergence point between art, literature and meaningfulness to create a product that changes society as you may know it.

We love stories. We create them, and we enjoy reading them. We want to give the world a story that updates and renews the purpose in life of mankind by sharing our message to any human in the Earth. Will you help us spread this word?

We are a vertical project.

And it's not that we're always looking up, thinking about growing. That too.

When authors publish a book, they think about turning that book into a series. In Joetagoinst, we want to go vertical, not horizontal in our production. We want to create more products, therefore, create a value. In the end, we believe that the essence of each book, each written piece, can be amplified, taken to every corner of the world in different languages, formats and media. When a book becomes the idea of thousands of people from every country, race and diversity in the world, then we know that our vertical project works.

"Create a story that would enhance the wellbeing of people."

We find beauty in stories, and at Joetagonist, we believe it should be appreciated by everyone, even those with the greatest difficulty. That's why we're a publisher committed to inclusion and integrity, and our books are tailored to different problems that some people face.

Specific formats for people with dyslexia is one of our first efforts to make our books accessible to everyone. In addition, in this way, we recreate value by multiplying the reach that the beauty of that book will have.

Why Joetagonist?

Well, it's not complicated. "Joe-", from Joseph, and "–tagonist", from protagonist. Now, let's go into detail.

Have you read our books? You should. The protagonist, Joseph (here's the origin) goes through countless adventures in each of our books. In "Joseph and the Seven Swords" your thrilling story will begin and who knows where Joseph's paths will lead us... it will surely you.

DLSX EDITION